COURT OF SHADOWS

SHADOW FAE—BOOK ONE

C.N. CRAWFORD

For my son James, whose vivid imagination created the concept of Ruadan.

CHAPTER 1

*T*he vampire bared his fangs, and I knew we'd both be dead by the end of the night if I didn't get him out of here. I leapt over the bar with the speed of a hurricane wind, hurtling toward him. I slammed my fist into his skull—once, twice, three times. He staggered back, then collapsed. He'd fallen so easily I almost didn't feel a sense of victory, but I grinned down at him anyway. The colored lights of the bar stained his porcelain skin red.

I *had* to get him out of here.

I tried to project a calm I didn't feel. "Like I said," I purred, "a guy like you would be more comfortable in a hipster joint with arcade games and herbal cocktails. You can talk about synthwave or whatever there. Move along. *Now.*" I may have screamed the last word. A sense of urgency was taking over.

It was at that point, I realized that everyone in the bar had stopped talking and were all staring at me over their pints. A pop song crackled through the speakers, and the neon sign in the window flickered on and off. Otherwise, silence shrouded us.

Easy, Arianna. Easy. I stood over the fallen vampire, holding up my hands. "Nothing to see here, folks! Just an ordinary Friday night kerfuffle."

I loosed a long sigh. Two thin hawthorn stakes jutted from my messy bun, ready for the vampire's heart, but I restrained myself. My boss would flip his shit if he saw me beating up customers—again. And I definitely wasn't supposed to kill people—even if they were undead—in front of a crowd. Rufus frowned upon things like that in his establishment.

You can take the girl out of the gladiator arena....

It was just unfortunate that the vampire had made the serious error of trying to bite me.

As soon as this guy had stumbled into our bar, I'd known he was trouble. In fact, I'd immediately assessed three important things about him.

One, his luxurious Viking beard had told me he was a hipster—not to mention his neon clothing, reminiscent of children's wear in the early 1980s. Whenever guys dressed like him decided to slum it in the Spread Eagle, it usually went down badly with the regulars.

Two, his staggering gait and furrowed brow had told me that he was a mean, sloppy drunk. Given the exceptional alcohol tolerance levels of vampires, he must have drunk his weight in craft beers tonight.

Three, and worst of all, he was a supernatural.

I cocked my head at him as he lay on the floor. He

might even be old enough that the medieval Norseman beard was actually authentic. Supernaturals like him—like me—were outlawed these days. We had to fly under the radar if we wanted to live. Too bad this one was too stupid to keep a low profile. Four years of executions and assassinations, and this fucker had just brazenly walked into our bar, flashing his fangs around.

As the patrons turned back to their pint glasses, pretending to ignore us, I frowned at the hipster-vampire. Dazed, he still lay on the beer-stained floor, but he'd managed to push himself up onto his elbows. The undead bastards didn't stay down for long. His pale eyes were trained on me, possibly recognizing my own magic.

Ciara, my oldest friend, crept over to us, her brown eyes wide. Her hand was clamped over her grin. I could tell she was stopping just short of clapping her hands. "Oh my goodness, Arianna. You punched him. Do you see his fangs?" She had a sweet but unfortunate tendency to idolize supernaturals, like we were some kind of celebrities. After all, there weren't many of us around these days. "A real, live vampire," she whispered, pointing at him.

"I can hear you," the vamp slurred, now rising to his feet. He staggered closer. "Little girl."

"I need to get him out of here," I muttered. And I had to do it without using any of my magic. You never knew who was watching, ready to turn you in.

Now, my new Viking friend's gaze was locked on

Ciara. Red flashed in his eyes. He was after blood tonight, and she was clearly an easier target than me. It didn't help that she was wearing a T-shirt featuring a male model with fangs poking from pouty lips. She gods-damned loved vampires.

"I know your game, little girl." The vampire licked his fangs, swaying on his feet. "You read your little books about teenagers falling in love with thousand-year-old vamps. Our skin is supposed to sparkle like a unicorn's arse, right? And you all get a happy ending. Wrong. Those books are crap. Come with me, and I'll teach you about reading real literature. Hemingway, Kerouac, Bukowski—"

His monologue was cut off by the sight of the thin stake I'd pulled out of my hair. I twirled it between my fingers, and the vampire seemed hypnotized by the movement.

I smiled at him. "Now that you're quiet, let's get one thing straight. I will not have you slandering romance books in my bar." Technically, it wasn't my bar, but that was beside the point. This arsehole thought he was going to feed on Ciara. And moreover, I would not tolerate anyone banging on about Bukowski. "I'd like to just get back to the shots of Johnny Walker I was drinking before you came in, and I don't want to have to keep punching you. I'd prefer not to get your blood on my new miniskirt. So run along. I'm pretty sure an ironic meth-trailer-themed bar just opened up a few blocks away." I leaned closer, arching an eyebrow. "It seems more your scene."

Despite the arse-kicking I'd just given him and the stake in my hand, he seemed unfazed.

He stumbled toward Ciara. "I think I'd be more comfortable if your friend came with me."

I gave him a hard shove, and he staggered back.

The door swung open, and a second vamp came in —this one in a visor, a handlebar mustache, and a pink bow tie. Had someone told them we had a sale on ukuleles or something?

I had to get them out of here. The last thing I wanted was for the Spread Eagle to attract the spell-slayers' attention for harboring supernaturals.

I flashed the two vamps a dark smile. "No supernaturals allowed in here. No supernaturals allowed *anywhere*. Those are the rules. You've got ten seconds to leave this bar," I said sweetly, while calculating all the ways I could kill them. "Or I might start getting angry. And you don't want that to happen."

Viking Vamp snorted, then his irises flared with red. The air seemed to thin around us. "And what the fuck are you, pretty thing? You're not human."

My blood chilled. I couldn't let anyone overhear him saying that.

He snatched a whisky bottle—my whisky bottle—from the bar, his movements lightning fast. Then, he jabbed a finger in my face. "You're not supposed to be here, either. I think I just might tell the spell-slayers on you. Tick tock. Your time is running out, pretty lady. But give me a look at those gorgeous tits of yours and I might keep your secret."

Rage surged. And then, as I registered the word "spell-slayers," dread slithered up my spine.

Okay. I was done being nice. Now he had to die.

There was only one thing in London scarier than me, and that was the spell-slayers. The fae assassins haunted London's streets in dark cloaks, blending into the night sky like smoke. They terrorized humans and magical creatures alike, ruling the city with the points of their blades, silently slaughtering in the shadows. No one was supposed to look them in the eye, or speak to them, or breathe in their direction. But we all owed them a tithe from our paychecks. Protection money, they called it. They were no better than a magical mafia. In short, they were the worst. I hated them and feared them in equal measure.

I narrowed my eyes at the vamps. "You want me to believe you're brave enough to attract the attention of the spell-slayers? And risk your own necks? Bollocks. You're supposed to be locked up in a magical realm with all the other supernaturals, not roaming London's streets. I'm now four seconds away from dragging you outside and staking you."

Truth was, I'd stake them whether or not they left willingly. I couldn't risk them turning me in.

I didn't really have time for too many mental calculations, because the next thing I knew, Viking Vamp was lunging for Ciara again, fangs bared.

Fast—maybe faster than I should have—I pivoted around him, pointing my stake at his neck. I wasn't supposed to move too quickly; humans were slow and sluggish. But the sight of him attacking Ciara sent my blood racing, and instinct kicked in.

I pressed the stake against his jugular. Then, I stood on my tiptoes, whispering into his ear. "I know a stake to the neck won't kill you. But I will make it hurt when I jam it into your throat and wiggle it round. Then I'll kill you."

Something sharp jabbed into my back, stopping me in my tracks. A quick glance over my shoulder told me that his friend, Visor Vamp, was holding a knife to my back.

"Drop the stake, darling!" said Visor Vamp.

Baleros's third law of power: Always let your enemy underestimate you.

I dropped the stake. I held up my hands as if I were surrendering, adding in a bit of trembling for good measure.

Then, when I felt the point of the knife retreat a little, I pivoted, slamming my elbow into his nose. I brought up my knee into his crotch—three brutal cracks to the groin. Vamps might not be alive, but they were still sensitive in the usual places. As he bent forward, I twisted his arm, forcing him to the ground. I snatched the knife from his hand at the same time. Then, I pointed it at his neck.

My lips curled in a mocking smile. "You still want to play?"

Now, at last, the vamps had the good sense to look scared. Apart from a warbling pop song, the room had gone silent again.

Viking Vamp held up his hands. "We'll leave."

I pulled the blade away from the other's neck. As he straightened, he leaned in close, breathing in my ear. "The spell-slayers will be coming for you."

At that, an icy tendril of dread coiled through my chest.

I watched as the two vamps skulked out of the bar.

I jammed my hand into the pocket of my miniskirt, and I pulled out a lollipop. Cherry, with gum in the center. Nothing like crystalized sugar to calm the nerves. I popped it in my mouth, staring at the door.

Ciara grinned. "Well geez Louise, this has been a heck of an evening." She'd lived in the UK for at least ten years now and still hadn't lost her thick American accent. "I haven't been this excited since my Aunt Starlene drew a clown on my bedroom wall to ease my loneliness."

"It's not over." There'd been something too cocky about those vamps, and their parting shot had told me everything I needed to know. I'd heard of some supernaturals acting as informants to the spell-slayers. Supernatural narcs. Maybe that was how these two idiots had managed to stay alive, biting humans like Ciara with impunity. "Can you cover the bar while I'm out?"

"No problem."

I had a pair of vampires to kill.

CHAPTER 2

I snatched my stake off the floor, then my backpack. I never went anywhere without it. My bug-out bag had everything I might need in an emergency: a headlamp, a lighter with aerosolized deodorant for smelling nice or lighting things on fire, medical supplies, a water bottle, cherry lip gloss, fresh knickers, a shortwave radio, ropes, assorted lollipops, duct tape, and a shitload of knives. Never say I wasn't prepared.

The door creaked as I pushed through it into the night air. A sooty bridge arched over the Spread Eagle, where pigeons made their home in the shadows. They cooed above me.

I tossed my lollipop in a rubbish bin. I didn't like to kill things with sweets in my mouth.

Shivering a little in the misty air, I scanned the dark streets under the bridge until I saw movement. The two vamps were moving toward the Tower—the seat of spell-slayer power. I wouldn't let them get any closer to its walls.

I trailed behind them over the damp, cobbled road, moving silently. A light rain misted over my skin, curling my lavender hair.

Quickening my pace, I drew the hawthorn stakes from my hair, holding one in each hand like a pair of daggers. My pulse raced, heart quickening with the thrill of the hunt. I had them in my sights, and I wasn't letting them get anywhere.

When I'd come up behind them, I crooned, "Hey, vamps."

They whirled, and I slammed my stakes into their hearts. And just like that, the fight was over.

Baleros's sixth law of power: Crush your enemies mercilessly.

Their eyes went wide, but within seconds, they had crumbled to piles of ash on the pavement. Rain dampened their blackened remains.

I pulled my stakes from the ash and wiped them off with a tissue from my bag. As I did, I lifted my eyes to the medieval fortress before me. Once, it had simply been known as the Tower of London. Now, people called it the Institute. It was the one place the spell-slayers hadn't outlawed magic. Even from here, I could see its walls and towers brimming with sorcery. Pale blue light streamed from the stony spires into the skies, and a moat of golden light surrounded the entire structure.

The spell-slayers claimed they'd outlawed magic to

keep the peace. They said that the apocalyptic wars twenty years ago—the ones between angels, fae, and demons—were forever at risk of erupting again. They said all supernaturals should remain segregated and locked in magical realms. Apparently, only the fae nobility were capable and worthy of remaining neutral among the human world. Everyone else was an animal, you see.

But I knew how the spell-slayers really thought. Magic was power, and they wanted it all for themselves. I hated them with an intensity that rivaled the brilliance of their gleaming spires.

I turned, walking back to the Spread Eagle. As I did, I tucked the hawthorn stakes back into my hair. I'd rid myself of that threat quickly enough. So why did I still feel that eerie sense of dread hanging over me?

When I slipped back into the bar, I found that another grim hush had overtaken the place, and my heart started to race.

I scanned the room until I figured out why.

When my gaze landed on a fae male in the corner, my blood began roaring in my ears.

I glimpsed a sweep of black hair under his cowl. The neon lights of the bar flashed over olive skin and vibrant green eyes. His broad shoulders took up half the booth, and an opening in his cloak revealed leather armor underneath. I had no doubt that every inch of his body was muscled and strapped with weapons. He held himself with a preternatural stillness, gazing at me like a snake about to strike. My stomach dropped.

Fae nobility, and a spell-slayer. Like so many of his kind, he was shockingly beautiful and terrifying at the same time. Under his stare, I felt uncharacteristically self-conscious in my bargain-basement miniskirt that was just a little too short. Of course, spell-slayers like him wanted everyone else to feel like crap. They lived to dominate and terrify. They'd mastered messing with people's heads.

And right now, I was certain he'd come for me, even if I'd tried to be careful.

If I turned and ran now, it would confirm my guilt, and he'd be after me instantly.

My gaze slid to the bar, where Ciara was trying to act natural, although her hands were shaking as she pulled a pint.

Rufus, our boss, now stood by her side. The presence of the spell-slayers had unnerved him, too, and I could see sweat droplets beading at the edges of his graying hair. Ciara and Rufus weren't even supernaturals, and the slayer still scared the crap out of them.

Rufus met my gaze, his eyes flicking wide open. The strained look on his face said, *Get the hell over here. Now.*

Swallowing hard, I crossed to him. I watched as he pulled our most expensive bottle of wine—which, let's be honest, was something he'd picked up from Tesco, simply labeled *French Red Wine.* Staring across the bar at the spell-slayer, he poured a glass.

I cast a quick glance at myself in the mirror behind Rufus. Straight eyebrows, high cheekbones, amber eyes. The only thing that might have marked me as a supernatural was the pale lavender shade of my hair, but plenty of humans dyed their hair bright colors these days. My fae canines and pointed ears only emerged when I thought my life was in danger, which didn't happen often. In other words, I could pass for human. Maybe he'd come for the vampires, instead?

"Take these over to him," whispered Rufus. "Tell him it's our best wine. Tell him it's on the house. Tell him we'll give him money. Tell him—" His eyes suddenly narrowed. "You didn't happen to see anything unusual tonight, did you?" He was still pouring the wine, and it spilled over the rim, pooling on the bar like blood.

I loosed a long sigh. I often found Rufus staring at the blank walls in his office, listlessly licking his yogurt spoon over and over. I honestly had no idea how someone like him had survived the apocalypse at all.

"Nothing unusual." I gently took the bottle from his hand. Might as well not give the guy a complete heart attack.

"Don't look him in the eyes," Rufus hissed, his eyes wide.

My gaze flicked back to the spell-slayer, and my stomach leapt as I realized his eyes were still on me. My throat went dry. There was no way in hell I was bringing him wine.

I was quickly realizing there was no way out of this situation without fighting a spell-slayer. And I knew only too well how vicious they could be.

"Actually, Rufus ... I'm not feeling so well."

"You what?" He sounded incredulous.

"Lady stuff."

"Oh." He fell silent. Apparently, that topic was more terrifying than the spell slayer.

"Gotta run. I'll see you tomorrow." I cast a quick glance at Ciara as I headed for the door. She was the only one around who knew I was a demi-fae. Baleros—my former gladiator master—had once assigned her to tend to my wounds between matches in the arena. Ciara and I had slept in the same cage for years. She knew my dreams and my nightmares. She knew why the scent of roses made me sick. She knew almost everything about me.

Almost.

As soon as I'd slipped outside into the damp air, I shoved my hand into my bug-out bag, rummaging around until I found my iron knife, sheathed in leather. I hated having to use iron. It was poisonous to fae like me, but it was the only way to hurt a spell-slayer.

Then, I pulled out my mobile and called Ciara.

"Arianna," she answered immediately, whispering into the phone. "He's still here. And now there's another one, with violet eyes. I've heard of him. He's the one they call the Wraith. He moves like wind in the night and slaughters silently in the shadows. I think he's the Devil himself."

"Very reassuring, thanks." She was always saying weird shit about the Devil. Pretty sure it was an American thing. Whatever the case, this was not wonderful news. "Just tell me when they're leaving."

"The Devil wears many faces," she hissed.

"I know. Just simmer down, friend. Look, I might have to fight them both. Just text me when they leave."

"Wait. Wait. If you make it home alive, put cat pee in front of your door, mixed with old cabbage."

"Is that supposed to ward off fae nobility?"

"Dunno, but Aunt Starlene put it outside our trailer to keep the police away after she threw an alligator at someone in a McDonald's parking lot. And she set bear traps." She scratched her cheek. "Also, she might have shot them, so ... that could have actually been the part that kept them out of our trailer."

"Thanks, Ciara. Gotta go." I shoved my mobile back in my pocket.

Dread bloomed in my chest.

Baleros's ninth law of power: Don't attack unless you're certain you can win.

I'd been trained by a spell-slayer. I knew how they fought.

As a gladiator, I'd often fought multiple opponents at once, taking them out within minutes. I had been the only female gladiator, and my stage name had been the Amazon Terror. The amount of blood I'd spilled had been more than enough to appease the crowds, and Baleros, because he was a complete prick, had fashioned special armor that emphasized my boobs. I'd been quite the attraction.

But spell-slayers were different than anyone I'd fought in the arena. They were ancient, disciplined, with centuries of exquisite training far beyond my own. My chances of winning in a fight against two of them were a little lower than my chances of sprouting wings and flying off to freedom. Before I flung my knife at them, I'd wait to see if they attacked first.

My phone buzzed, and I pulled it out to read the text.

They're leaving.

Adrenaline raced through my blood, and I dodged into an alleyway. It's not like I could really hide, though. Fae trackers like them would be able to smell me.

I quickened my pace, but I'd only gone a few steps before the hairs on the back of my neck stood on end. I could feel them watching me, and my pulse started racing out of control. A cold sweat dampened my brow.

How had they gotten here so fast?

I gripped the hilt of the knife hard, and I whirled.

A pit opened in my stomach at the sight of two cloaked spell-slayers standing just behind me. Frigid panic rippled up my spine.

CHAPTER 3

*T*he green-eyed one from the bar stepped closer, his gaze flicking up and down my body, as if he were assessing my worth. I felt goose-bumps rise on my skin.

But it was the other one who stopped my heart. Menacing shadows curled off him, like smoke from a funeral pyre. He was taller than the other, his shoulders broad and no doubt thickly muscled under his cloak. He gripped a dagger, red with blood that dripped onto the pavement. Drops of blood glistened on his cloak. Darkness breathed around him like a living thing, and I held my breath.

It was hard to look at him—the more I focused my eyes, the less distinct he seemed. The most salient thing about him was his piercing, violet eyes, which raised the hair on the back of my neck.

I took a step back. His magic was powerful—and unusual for a fae.

As they stared at me, I was mentally calculating the chances of taking them both on. It wasn't good, and worse, even if I managed to survive, it would mean the end of my life as I knew it. A fugitive permanently on the run from the spell-slayers.

"Hello, gents." I aimed for a casual tone, but it came out sounding strained.

"Hello, Arianna," said the one with green eyes.

My heart skipped a beat. He knew my name.

I licked my lips. "And to whom do I have the pleasure of speaking?"

"Aengus, Knight of the Shadow Fae."

The other one—the Wraith—said nothing.

Don't attack unless you're certain you can win.

The Wraith shifted, and I lost sight of him until he reappeared on the opposite side of Aengus. For a moment, the wind picked up his cowl, and I caught a better view of his eyes. His gaze held no emotion, just a cold detachment. And yet somehow, his glare slid through my bones. I felt like a pinned butterfly under his stare, completely helpless.

He shifted again, appearing on the other side of Aengus once more, before going completely still. Eerily still.

Whoever he was, he moved with a lethal, otherworldly grace. A shiver danced up my spine. He'd come out tonight for one reason and one reason only: to kill.

The Wraith's unnerving stillness ignited the most ancient parts of my brain with primal fear. Even if I couldn't see his face, his lethality was apparent. For the first time in years, real terror clenched my chest. I gripped my iron knife tighter.

I didn't see him coming, didn't catch the tensing of muscles that normally signaled an oncoming attack. Just the whoosh of wind, a blur of black, and the Wraith slammed my wrist against the brick wall behind me. The force felt like he'd cracked my bones, and I dropped the knife. He kicked it away, and it spun off down the alleyway.

So. This was going well so far.

The Wraith flickered away from me again, now behind Aengus.

Bollocks. The other knives were packed deep within my bug-out bag, and now all I had access to were the hawthorn stakes in my hair. Hawthorn wouldn't kill them, but jammed in the right places, it would certainly slow them down. In the future, I'd be strapping iron knives all over myself.

Assuming I got out of here alive.

Aengus stared at me. "Arianna," he said. "You're a demi-fae. You're supposed to be in a fae realm, but you're not. You should have submitted to our laws long ago. Do you know what we do to outlaws like you?"

My blood ran cold. "What makes you say that I'm fae?" I asked.

"We can smell our kind." Aengus's brow furrowed. "If you can be considered our kind at all. Your fae scent isn't noble, even if it is alluring."

My entire body had gone rigid with tension, and I

19

reviewed all my combat lessons in hyper-speed. "Two on one isn't really a fair fight, is it?"

A half-smile curled Aengus's beautiful lips. "Who said anything about fairness?"

That was all the warning I got before he lunged for me. In the next moment, his hand was around my neck, but I slammed my forearm into his, knocking his hand off my throat.

Baleros's fourth law of power: Always anticipate your enemy's actions.

My gaze darted to the Wraith, and I realized I had absolutely no idea how to predict his actions, because what the hell?

But Aengus was clearer. By the tensing of his muscles, I knew he was about to strike again.

He swung for me. Despite his speed, I managed to catch his fist in my palm. I twisted his arm, then gripped him by the back of his hair, driving his face down hard into my knee. *Crack.*

Crush your enemies completely.

I yanked out a stake, ready to plunge it into his back, but he was up again within moments.

Unusually strong, even for a fae.

His fist slammed me hard in the jaw, dizzying me. It had been a long time since I'd taken a hard hit, and I was out of practice.

Still, I recovered fast enough. Before he got the chance to hit me again, I thrust my stake hard into his neck. Blood spurted. It wasn't iron, so it wouldn't kill him, but he wouldn't be getting up any time soon.

I pulled the second stake from my hair, ready to take on the Wraith.

Except—he wasn't there anymore. I didn't even see him moving for me, I just felt the force of his body twisting my arm, spinning me in the other direction. He slammed me into the wall of the alley. The cold stone bit into my cheek. He had me completely pinned, his powerful body pressing against mine. Before, I'd sensed something like indifference from him. Now, given the ferocity of his grip, it was a little more like cold-blooded wrath. Firm muscles pressed against me, completely rooting me in place.

I wasn't used to *anyone* being able to dominate me, and hot fury—mixed with fear—gripped me. Maybe the Wraith really *was* the Devil himself.

This was it. Baleros had no rule to describe this situation, because I was never supposed to let myself get pinned like this in the first place. My mind raced wildly as I waited for the pain that would usher me into the afterlife.

But instead of an iron blade severing my jugular, I felt the searing pain of magic at the nape of my neck.

Then, the force of his body disappeared.

When I whirled around again, both fae were gone. I stared only at the shadowy, cobbled street. I put my hand to my heart, catching my breath. And as I did, I realized I was clutching a piece of paper. I wasn't even clear how I'd gotten the paper, but as I unfolded it—with shaking hands—I found a note inscribed in unexpectedly feminine looping letters.

We will return for you. You will join the Shadow Fae, or you will die on the execution block.

What in the name of seven hells?

Exhaustion burned through me. They'd left me alive, and I'd survived the fight—but I had no idea why. Fear scratched at the back of my mind. Somehow, the mystery of whatever they had planned for me was more unnerving than the idea of death itself.

I crossed out of the alleyway, shaking all over.

The sight of the Institute's blazing spires sent a shiver of admiration up my spine. I hated my reaction to the place. It was a symbol of oppression, of domination and conquest, and I couldn't help but be awed by the vibrant display of magic.

And now—for reasons I couldn't fathom—they wanted me to join them behind its walls.

CHAPTER 4

I woke curled in a ball on top of a pile of laundry and lollipop wrappers, certain I'd just snapped out of a terrible nightmare. It was still night, and a quick glance at my phone told me I'd only been asleep for a half hour. In fact, I was still wearing my rumpled miniskirt.

I rubbed my eyes, flicking on my phone's light.

It took me nearly a full minute to remember what had happened earlier, and then it all came crashing down on me like a storm wave. The vampires, the spell-slayers. The disturbing and unfamiliar feeling of being helpless, my body pinned against a wall. The threat that I could either join them or die.

Something about the night—maybe the magical spell they'd applied to my neck—had exhausted me so much that I'd just collapsed as soon as I'd returned home to my East London shithole, completely disoriented.

I scurried over to my bug-out bag, rifling through my last medical supplies and road flares until I found an iron knife with a leather sheath. I strapped the sheath around my thigh.

Now, adrenaline pumped in my veins, and I yanked open the door, heading for the communal bathroom. Rufus didn't pay me much, and until I saved up, I was squatting with ten other people in an abandoned apartment.

I shared the bathroom with all my house-mates, including a fifty-year-old man who called himself Uncle Darrell and a woman who permanently wore a bathing cap and asked anyone within earshot if she could borrow hand lotion. I donated a bottle to her at least once a week, though I'd rather pull out my own teeth than learn what she did with it.

At the end of the hall, I slammed through the door into the bathroom. I tried to ignore Uncle Darrell, who was hanging out in a towel and flip-flops on the edge of the bathtub. I often found him here in the middle of the night.

"Have I ever told you what I do on the weekends?" he began.

Please don't.

"I connect to the power of the earth," he went on. "Bury my manhood in the fresh forest soil."

Vomit. "How about we don't have this discussion?"

"My shaman says it's gotta be the whole ballsack and not just the shaft. It's quite the commitment, going out into nature."

"Could you not just use a potted plant in the comfort of your own living room?" No idea why I was prolonging this conversation.

He scratched his chin. "I'm not sure that would work, but I'll try it."

Again—how had these people survived an apocalypse?

I rummaged around in the cabinet below the sink, while Uncle Darrell relayed the mild embarrassment he'd felt when a badger caught him balls-deep in Mother Earth. At last, I found a hand mirror, and I pulled it out.

I turned around, using it to look at the back of my neck. And there, glowing on my spine, was a faint, golden rune—a fae mark that I couldn't read.

My hands shook as I dropped the mirror on the side of the sink. I didn't know exactly what it meant, but if I had to guess, the spell-slayers would use it to track me, and it might explain my weird fatigue. So, the Wraith hadn't been kidding when he'd said I'd have to join them or die.

I wouldn't give them the chance.

"You ain't listening, are ya'?" yelled Uncle Darrell.

"Scrotum. Dirt. Got it."

I raced back to my dark room. My heart thumping, I slammed through the door.

My emergency backpack lay by the door, and I frantically unzipped it. I retrieved the headlamp, clamping it on my head.

Then, I found my sharpest knife. I was quickly

developing a plan. I'd cut off the tracking mark, then I'd escape London. Maybe I'd go to Edinburgh, take on a new identity, dye my hair black or something.

Kneeling on the floor, I pulled the silver dagger from my bag, and I brought it to the skin on the back of my neck, pressing the blade into my nape.

"I wouldn't do that if I were you." Cold fear shot through my blood. I knew that voice—the lilting aristocratic fae accent. A voice from my most violent nightmares. And the sweet scent of rosewater—a smell from my nightmares.

I didn't think this day could actually get any worse.

I turned, and the light from my headlamp beamed over a man I'd hoped never to see again. Already, I was shaking at the sight of him. How had he even gotten in here?

Of course, he'd once been a spell-slayer, too. He knew how to move in the shadows.

Even though he was a member of the fae nobility, he'd cultivated a scruffy look. Baggy woolen trousers with thick navy and white stripes, a handlebar mustache, a bit of stubble. Pink cheeks, and eyes a deep copper, flecked with gold. He looked like an impoverished Victorian clown, but I knew the truth. He was actually a noble fae who viewed himself as king of the miscreants. Lord of the monsters. He'd created a world for himself where he was treated like an emperor. Like a god, even.

It was all part of his act. He wanted everyone outside the arena to underestimate him. I'd never make that mistake—which is why I didn't try to jam my knife into his eye socket right then and there.

"What are you doing here?" I spat out. The bastard already haunted my thoughts. Now he'd invaded my room?

He shrugged. "I've been watching you, of course. I'd never let anyone as valuable as you out of my sight. A delicate beauty and a ruthless killer in one perfect package. The Amazon Terror. I've missed you terribly."

My jaw clenched. He was already getting to me. "I'm not a ruthless killer anymore. Those days ended when the spell-slayers shut down your arena."

He arched his eyebrows. "Not ruthless? Then what did you do to those two poor vampires?"

I fell silent. I had no desire to engage with his mind games. He obviously wanted something, and I just needed him to get to the point.

He frowned at the mess in my tiny room. "Well, it certainly appears that you've made the most of your life since you left my care. Impressive what you've done with the place. And I very much like the look of you in a headlamp."

I narrowed my eyes, still gripping the knife. "Funny," I purred. "I must have missed out on a few housekeeping lessons when I was living on a dirt floor underground. The conditions in my cage never seemed to bother you. In fact, I thought you liked me surrounded by filth. Keep the monsters in their place, right?"

Okay. He was definitely getting to me. Of course he was. He was Baleros.

"What do you want?" I barked, eager to get this over with.

"I have a task for you," he said.

I took a deep breath to calm myself. I wouldn't let him see that he was rattling me.

"Why would I do anything for you?" I pressed the point of my knife to my fingertip, twirling it. "How about I stab you in the throat instead, then run your body full of iron nails?"

"I don't think so, Arianna." His face still betrayed no emotion. "You know better than to attack someone who would slaughter you within moments. But I must say, I'm surprised you're not living with Ciara. Wouldn't she be safer in your company?"

My stomach dropped. Why was he bringing up Ciara? He didn't give a shit about Ciara. As my helper, she'd been a servant to a slave—the lowest of the low. I was surprised he even knew her name.

"My dear Arianna," he said. "I know you've internalized all my laws. All of them apart from the second one: Caring for others makes you weak. You have a pathetic tendency to grow attached to anyone who shows you the smallest bit of kindness."

My blood turned to ice, and my legs started shaking. I could no longer control my voice. "What have you done with Ciara?" Fury snapped through my nerve endings. It was taking every ounce of my restraint not to lunge for him right now. "What do you want from me?"

He rose, towering over me. Then, he pulled out a mobile phone. He swiped the screen, and an image came up—Ciara, tied to a chair in a bare room. At the sight of her, icy dread tightened its grip around my heart.

A light shone on her, and tears streamed down her face. She looked like she was screaming, rattling the chair in her panic, but a gag bound her mouth. Her vampire shirt was torn at the shoulder, as if she'd struggled.

Rage shook me.

Baleros shoved the phone back into his pocket. "She's in my care until you get me what I want."

"What the fuck do you want?" I gritted out through clenched teeth.

"Something called the World Key."

Wrath spiraled in my mind. "The *what?*"

"You met a few spell-slayers tonight, didn't you? Of course, they recruit anyone who fights well enough. I knew you'd fight well, my little monster."

Understanding crashed into me like a freezing wave. "You turned me in, didn't you?"

A slow shrug. "I need you to join their ranks. I need the World Key, and the Institute has it. Those two slayers you met marked you, didn't they? They're going to recruit you. And you're going to go with them willingly. Find the key and steal it for me. A spell-slayer known as Ruadan possesses it. It's a simple task."

It was taking everything in my power not to attack him right now. "You set me up. You set all of this up."

My rage didn't faze him. "If you don't give the key to me within two weeks, I will feed sweet little Ciara to my dragon. When you have it, send a message through one of the Tower's ravens. I'll come find you."

He didn't have a dragon, but that was beside the point. He'd kill Ciara brutally, and he'd send me the photos. I knew that much.

Violence simmered in my blood, and I gritted my teeth. "What do you want this key for?"

He cocked his head, studying me. "A state of chaos is like unmolded clay, ready to be shaped by our wills. Anarchy is the opportunity to remake the world the way we want it."

I was in no mood for his lessons now. "Just don't do anything to Ciara, and I'll get you your bloody key."

He wagged a finger in my face. "But do not cross me, my Amazon Terror. I have eyes within the Institute, and if you betray me, I will destroy Ciara. Then you will die with the knowledge that you killed her."

I'd get him his key. But as soon as Ciara was safe, I'd find a way to kill him. The more power a man like him had, the worse the world would be.

CHAPTER 5

 locked the door to my room from the inside and dropped to the floor, trembling. I picked up my phone to dial Ciara's number, but it went straight to voicemail.

How had Baleros reacted so quickly after the spell-slayers had found me? How had he even known about it?

While my mind was whirling over all the possibilities, a powerful force slammed against the door. Another hit, and the wood splintered, fracturing into my room. I leapt to my feet. On the other side of the broken door stood Aengus and the Wraith, the latter's body shrouded in tendrils of darkness. Having just decimated my door, the Wraith pulled back his fist.

My stomach curdled again. There was something entirely unnerving about the shadows surrounding him. They writhed like ghostly serpents, sending chills rippling over my skin.

"You really could have just knocked like a normal person," I said, composing myself.

The Wraith didn't answer. He just reached through the broken wood to turn the doorknob. His cold, violet gaze promised savagery if I crossed him. In short, we were off to a wonderful start.

As he stepped into the room, Aengus gave a slow shrug. "Apologies. Something seems to have made him uneasy. He doesn't speak, so his motives are anyone's guess."

Oh, lovely. A voiceless, psychotic fae who I'm pretty sure wants to gut me.

Aengus frowned at me. "What in the name of the gods are you wearing on your head? Is this a gutter fae accessory?"

"It's a headlamp. It's practical. Our electricity doesn't work so well. And if you're trying to irritate me by calling me a gutter fae, it won't work. I've been called far worse by better people."

The Wraith sniffed the air like an animal scenting prey. When his eyes met mine again, he snarled. For one terrible moment, I was certain he was going to rip my head off. Then, he backed away again, and I loosed the breath I'd been holding.

I narrowed my eyes at Aengus. "I stabbed you in the neck. Even if it wasn't iron, how did you recover so fast?"

He shoved his hands in his pockets, amusement curling his lips. "Ah, but you're a gutter fae. The Mor like us aren't quite so easily defeated."

I let him see my dramatic eye roll. The Mor were an ancient race of the fae. I didn't know much about them, but I was quickly getting the impression that their arrogance and snobbery vastly outweighed the allure of their beauty.

"Right. Sounds like a load of bollocks," I said. "I'm going to hazard a guess that you have exceptionally skilled healers in your pretty little palace. The noble Mor must need them a lot, considering you managed to get stabbed while ganging up on a solitary female gutter fae."

Aengus shrugged. "Your appearance threw me off, and I didn't want to hurt you. I don't enjoy killing beautiful women."

I nodded. "You're good with murdering the ugly ones, though, right? Aren't you the gentleman."

"Since you're apparently so perceptive, Arianna, do you know why we're here?"

I touched the back of my neck. "I found a mark you left. Honestly, it was pretty hard to miss." I couldn't tell him the information Baleros had passed on to me, so I had to act natural. Or, as natural as one could act after two fae warriors busted down the door to your room and insulted your headlamp. "And your chatty friend left a note about joining you. You'll have to fill me in on the rest."

"The Shadow Fae have decided to recruit you as a novice. If you can survive the first trial," he continued, "you'll be matched with one of six knights as your mentor."

"Matched?"

"You'll spend day and night with your mentor, learning to be…." He gestured at my room. "Better than you are now."

I cocked my head. "Quite the intense relationship."

"Arianna." His silky voice caressed my skin. "Living with us is surely a step up from how you're living now."

He was insulting me, but his voice promised seduction, and somehow, I forgot to take offense. Pretty men were annoying that way.

And maybe he had a point. A musty smell hung heavily over my apartment—if it could even be called an apartment. It was a single room, with a hot plate where I cooked my dinner and a tiny sink. I had no bed. I slept on the floor—a relic of my old gladiator days.

I blinked at the mess around me. Crisp wrappers, an empty bottle of Jack, some of my dirty clothes. Cleaning wasn't really my forte. But that's what happens when you spend six years in a cage, I guess.

I crossed my arms. "Considering I'm a gutter fae slob—why exactly would you recruit me?"

He took another step closer, and he leaned down to whisper. "As you pointed out, you managed to stab me." His voice warmed the shell of my ear. "Normally, I'd never let a female get that close to me unless we were engaged in a more enjoyable activity."

I took a step away from him. Was he here to recruit me, or seduce me?

"You will compete with the other novices," he

continued. "And probably die. But if you don't, you will be given the chance to become a Knight of the Shadow Fae, like us."

"A Knight of the Shadow Fae? Is that what you call yourselves? Everyone else says 'spell-slayer.'"

"We don't like that term."

"Of course not," I said. "It sounds unpleasant. What if I say no?"

Aengus quirked a smile. "Then you'll die, obviously. You're an outlaw. You have no rights."

"I'm not sure I like my options."

Surprise flickered in Aengus's green eyes. "We normally don't even bother with your type, but it was *his* idea. I'm not sure why. My companion here typically hates fae like you."

"Fae like me? You mean, someone with an actual personality?"

"No," said Aengus. "From what we've seen, you're a rule-breaking, impulsive slob prone to heavy drinking and undignified bar brawls. Your entire existence literally serves no purpose."

"I feel like there might have been an insult somewhere in there, but I can't quite put my finger on it."

"You're being given a chance at greatness, to live in a fortress and eat the food of knights, and you'd prefer to live like an animal, in a room covered in empty bottles and crisp packets?"

"Animals don't eat crisps or drink from bottles." I narrowed my eyes to deliver my final, stinging retort. "Animals don't even have hands."

"Quite clever for someone wearing a headlamp because they couldn't pay their bills."

"You play your cards right, I might get you your own headlamp someday. If you could see in the dark, maybe you could avoid the stakes flying at your neck."

This was all for show. For Ciara's sake, I was going with them no matter what, but it would perhaps raise suspicions if I just gave in without putting up a bit of a fight. After all, I was clearly an undignified, bar-brawling slob whose life served no purpose, and it might look a little suspect if I suddenly cared about achieving greatness.

I nodded at the Wraith. Shadows writhed around him. "And you're telling me I could end up roommates with Good Time Charlie over here?"

A slow shrug. "It's a possibility."

A distinctly unpleasant possibility, but Ciara's life was at stake. "Why did you let me come back here at all? Why not just take me from the street?"

"We need permission from Grand Master Savus before any outsiders can pass through our gates, and we knew you wouldn't be going far with the fatigue spell placed on you."

"Okay. So I room with you or die. I get it. What happens now?"

"Now, you come with us. If you can pass the threshold outside the Institute, you become a novice."

"The threshold? You mean the glowing moat thing?"

"Enough questions," said Aengus. "It's time to go."

I cast a nervous glance at the Wraith, whose cowl

covered most of his face. Still, I could tell by the rigid set of his shoulders that tension gripped him. I couldn't tell if that was from the state of my room, my status as a gutter fae, or if he'd had the misfortune to encounter Uncle Darrell and his ballsack anecdotes on the way in here. But whatever the case, the feel of his keenly intelligent eyes on me raised goosebumps on my skin. I was pretty sure he didn't miss much.

I was supposed to steal a key from one of these guys. What would someone like the Wraith do if one of his enemies stole something important from him? I didn't imagine it would be pretty.

Thinking of Ciara locked up in a cell somewhere, I knew I didn't have a choice. Ciara wasn't a warrior. She'd been raised in some backwater American hellhole by an aunt who beat the crap out of her, and I'm pretty sure she'd never once fought back. After we'd escaped our underground life with Baleros, Ciara had saved up to buy a set of soft toys that she placed around her bed at night for safety. She had one called Mr. Huggins that she cuddled whenever she had nightmares.

Now, she'd found herself stuck in a real life nightmare, and no amount of soft toy protectors would get her out of it.

I snatched my bug-out bag off the floor.

"You won't be needing your things," said Aengus. "The Institute will provide everything you need."

My jaw tightened. "I take this everywhere."

With a lightning-fast reflex, the Wraith snatched it

from me. He rifled through it. Then, he plucked out each knife from the bag and shoved it back at me. At least I had my emergency supplies and my lollipops. And duct tape, should things get really interesting with my roommate.

Most importantly, I still had the iron knife strapped to my thigh.

I scanned the room, grabbing a bottle of Jack on my way out the door. No way in hell was I leaving that behind.

CHAPTER 6

We approached the Institute, and I sucked in a deep breath.

What knowledge did they keep behind their ancient stone walls? What magical secrets and ancient teachings?

I pushed a strand of damp hair out of my eyes, staring up at the medieval tower as we moved closer.

After the angelic apocalypse decades ago, the world had descended into a dark period known as the Anarchy. Fae, demons, and humans battled to fill the power vacuum. In the end, humans agreed to let the fae nobility—these arseholes—act as enforcers. They were supposed to keep the peace. All other supernaturals were locked in magical realms.

And now? I'd find out exactly what secrets they'd been hoarding behind their walls.

We drew closer to the Institute. Its beaming spires and moat illuminated our bodies with blue and gold.

The ancient stone walls loomed above the Thames. A bridge spanned the moat of light, leading to a stone gatehouse with two stout towers.

A fortress, one that had stood here for over a thousand years, a symbol of human achievement and conquest—and now the fae had taken it over. They'd made it their own. When the humans had cut a deal with the Shadow Fae, had they realized they'd be submitting to them?

I couldn't help but wonder about what magical knowledge lurked behind those walls now that they'd turned it into the Institute. Whatever it was, I wanted it for myself. The spell-slayers were right—magic *was* power.

Weirdly, my stomach started rumbling with hunger. It was hardly the time to think about food, but I couldn't stop thinking about the lollipops in my backpack. I fought the nearly overwhelming impulse to pull them out now. I needed to act at least a *little* cool in front of the slayers.

My two new friends flanked me, and Aengus slid his green eyes to me. "Ruadan and I will cross the bridge. When we get to the other side, you set out for the gatehouse, too."

I froze. Oh, *bollocks*. The Wraith was Ruadan? The person I was supposed to steal a key from?

I swallowed hard. "Why doesn't Ruadan talk?"

Shadows slid around Ruadan, and I glanced at his hands—powerful hands that could crush a man's windpipe within seconds. This would not be easy.

I'd never hated Baleros more than I did at that moment.

"Don't worry about why he doesn't speak," said Aengus. "Just worry about staying alive in the next ten minutes. Have a look over the bridge as you start to cross. Your headlamp should illuminate things for you. Most recruits don't make it past the threshold."

I'd faced death often enough, and I gave him a shrug. "I'm not most recruits."

"Your cockiness is going to get you killed some day."

I flashed him a charming smile. "It hasn't yet. Now, are you going to give me a clue about what to expect?"

"No."

Of course not. That would be helpful.

Without another word, he and Ruadan turned and began crossing the bridge. Amber light from the moat gilded the two spell-slayers. I hated them for it, but the bastards looked like a pair of warrior gods as they crossed the bridge, swords slung over their backs.

And here I was, shivering in my crappy clothes and headlamp, clutching my weird bug-out bag of lollipops. *Delicious lollipops.* For reasons I couldn't explain, I *really* wanted them right now. Why the hells was I so hungry? I'd eaten an entire pizza for dinner.

Aengus and Ruadan reached the other side of the bridge, and they stood in the shadow of the gatehouse, just in front of a wooden door.

Tension rippled over me. I didn't like facing unknown enemies. Being unprepared was an enormous disadvantage. Whatever foe I was about to face, he was probably used to fighting fae like me, and I didn't yet know how he operated.

Slowly, I began crossing the bridge. As I did, I felt the magical light washing over my skin in a rush of euphoric tingles. It felt like sunshine after a long winter, mixed with peppermint oil. If it hadn't been for my hunger, I would have felt perfect.

A tug at my chest compelled me to look down at the moat. The white circle of illumination from my head-lamp pierced the river of golden light, and some of that euphoria dissolved. Under the golden magic, vibrant green grass grew around bones. Skulls, femurs, ribs … so *that* was what Aengus meant. What had happened to these recruits? When I strained my eyes, I thought I saw the faintest hints of green smudged on the skulls' teeth….

A shuffling behind me turned my head, and I whirled to find a pathetic creature standing on the bridge. A skeletal, cloaked figure, with tangled white hair poking from his hood. He looked half dead, his cheeks hollow, lips thin. Strangely, something green and pulpy was smeared across the lower half of his face, like someone had mashed up plants and rubbed it over his mouth.

I'd been expecting someone monstrous—a fae giant, maybe a creature with one eye and a giant wooden club. I'd fought men like that before. I'd never fought a creature who looked like he already had one foot in the grave. I almost felt sorry for him.

But Baleros had taught me well, and I knew better than to underestimate my opponents, even if they looked like death. After all, anyone I'd fought in the arena had found themselves facing off against a petite, lavender-haired girl. Most had underestimated me. And they'd all lost.

Mentally, I reviewed Baleros's lessons.

Assess surroundings. Learn weaknesses.

The figure stepped closer, and the hunger in the pit of my stomach intensified. I clutched my gut, suddenly ravenous, my mouth watering. Images danced in my head of pies, sandwiches—even Ciara's weird American spray cheese. My stomach rumbled. Why the hells was I thinking about food right now? I was supposed to be evaluating my opponent, and I was thinking of gods-damned spray cheese.

I frowned at him as he took a step closer, and I felt as if a yawning void were opening up between my ribs. I'd never been this ravenous before. Even when Baleros had taken my food away for a week at a time, and I was sure the ravening hunger would drive me mad, it hadn't been this intense. Maybe the grass would fill me....

Another step closer. I clutched my stomach, unable to think about anything but the piercing desire to fill my stomach with grass.

But—grass? What in the seven hells?

That's when I understood his power. I'd seen the stains on the teeth of the skulls. Like the Horseman of Famine who'd once walked this earth, this fae inspired

43

a feeling of starvation in a person. And then, a compulsive desire to eat moat grass. That's how the other recruits had died, chewing ravenously until their bodies gave out, drained of life.

I sniffed the air, catching the faintest hint of moss on him. He was a fae, like me. That meant he was particularly vulnerable to iron. Good thing I had the iron knife with me. I slid it out of the sheath on my leg. Ruadan really should have been more thorough.

I gritted my teeth, pushing the hunger out of my mind, and lunged for the creature. He dodged out of my way. Just a swirl of steam and a hiss of air, and he'd evaded my blade, reappearing on my other side.

Hunger gnawed at my gut.

I pivoted, lunging again, faster this time. But once again, he slipped away with just a hiss of air.

So he was fast, and the feeling of starvation was getting worse. Now, I could think of almost nothing except filling my belly with grass.

Focus, Arianna. Kill. Clearly, I couldn't defeat him through speed. I had to get him to let down his guard. I had to lure him to me.

Some fae—the worst kind—fed off the pain of others. If this one fed off hunger, I'd let him feast from me.

I went very still, forcing myself not to move even as I felt desperate need to fill my belly. As the sharp, gaping pain in my stomach intensified, I knew he was getting closer.

Oh gods, I needed to throw myself into the moat, to

stuff my mouth with grass and chew and chew until the hunger didn't hurt me anymore. I needed to fill my belly so desperately…. The grass was calling to me. The grass would fill me. Drool pooled in my mouth.

But I knew that way lay madness. If I jumped into the moat, I'd never make it out.

Assess weaknesses….

With each sharpening pain in my stomach, I was drawing him closer. This one fed off other people's hunger, but he was also driven by his own cravings.

Exploit the weaknesses.

Maybe I had a bit of an advantage over some of the other novices who'd fought him. I was used to this feeling. When Baleros had grown angry with me—if I hadn't earned him as much money as I was supposed to, or if I'd talked back—he'd lock me in a metal box. I'd go a full week with nothing but water. And the only way I hadn't lost my mind was that I'd retreated to my fantasy world, one I dreamt about at night: a bedroom in a palace, with one wall open to the air. A roaring river carved through a verdant valley below the window, where honeysuckle bloomed all around me. And curling over the floral scents in the air, the sweet smell of apples….

I had no idea where the image had come from, but my fantasy world often seemed more vivid to me than the real world. Right now, I could almost taste the bread—

A sharp stab of hunger ripped me in two. I sniffed the air. He was close enough, and I opened my eyes.

Go in for the kill.

This time, my blade was in his chest before he had a chance to dodge away.

The creature's body began to crack and desiccate before my eyes, his skin flaking off. He crumbled to dust before me, until nothing remained but his cloak.

The hunger receded from my belly, and I slid the knife back into its sheath.

When I crossed to the other side of the bridge, Ruadan and Aengus were waiting for me, lurking in the shadows before a wooden door.

"You survived," said Aengus.

Ruadan moved for me—so fast I didn't have the chance to react—and in the next moment, he was pressing me up against the stone wall. His forearm dug into my chest, and he bared his canines in a ferocious snarl. Panic tightened my lungs.

His cowl had fallen, and for the first time, his features came into focus. White-blond hair hung over his shoulders. Even in the moonlight, his skin looked golden, and shadows molded the striking planes of his face. If it weren't for the malice etched across his features, he'd actually be exquisitely beautiful.

He snarled, and the sound reverberated through my gut. Panic dug its claws into my chest.

By the shadows sliding in his eyes, I knew, then, he was part demon.

"What?" I spit out, horrified to realize that my legs were shaking. "I did what I was supposed to do."

He smelled like a pine forest. And something else,

too. The scent of seared air after lightning strikes—the smell of a powerful, dark magic.

His response was a hand up my skirt. He ripped the leather sheath off my thigh, and the force of it stung my skin.

Releasing me, he took my only weapon from me.

He glared at me for a moment, boxing me in to the stone wall. The wind toyed with his pale blond hair.

I let out a slow, shaky breath. "Usually I save up-the-skirt action for a third date, but since you've got such a sparkling personality...."

He simply pulled the cowl over his head, then pushed through the ancient wooden door. Stalking away from us, he disappeared into the shadows of the Institute's grounds.

Nice, friendly people here.

I suppressed a shudder. I'd fought many monsters in my time, but Ruadan was different. He ignited a primal sense of fear, stirring instincts far older than language. If I stole from him, I'd have two choices. Find a way to kill him, or spend the rest of my life hiding from him.

It would no longer just be Baleros haunting my nightmares. The Wraith would lurk there, too.

CHAPTER 7

hen we crossed through the gateway, we remained in the open air. Under a canopy of stars, I walked over the cobbled ground by Aengus's side. I had a general idea that two concentric, U-shaped walls formed the outermost fortifications of the Institute's grounds, and that we were walking between them. But I didn't have the full layout, yet.

As we walked, ancient stone walls loomed over either side of the path. My headlamp bounced over dark, narrow windows in the towering stone around us. Moss and vines grew all around.

I loosed a long breath, reviewing my situation. Ruadan had taken my knife, but it wasn't the end of the world. Baleros had taught me to turn the world around me into weapons. Furniture, brooms, glass bottles—all sort of objects could be used to maim or kill. I'd never be truly without a weapon.

As we walked, Aengus cast me a sharp glance. "You look ridiculous with that thing on your head."

"At least I can see." I bit my lip. "So, that was an interesting test. How many of those creatures do you sacrifice for your trials? And how do people kill them if we're not supposed to have weapons?"

"The gorta?" Aengus slid his gaze to me. "We've only sacrificed one so far. You weren't supposed to kill him. You were simply supposed to withstand the hunger and then walk on. You were the one who decided that the trial involved death. Now we have to get a new one, which will be a right pain in the arse."

Awkward. "Well, it involved death for all those recruits whose bones now decorate the moat. I wasn't about to let myself become one of them."

"Has anyone ever told you that you have a ruthless side?"

I flashed him my sweetest smile. *Oh, you have no idea.*

"Where did you learn to fight?" he asked, his eyes narrowing. "You look young for someone so skilled."

"I learned underground." And that was all the answer he was getting.

"I guess that explains the headlamp."

"Where are you taking me now?"

"To your temporary lodgings."

"And after tonight, I could end up with you or Ruadan?" I may have injected a bit of venom into his name, but he had seriously annoyed me so far.

49

"There are four other knights as well. I take it you don't like Ruadan."

"I'd call him interpersonally challenged, what with all the shadows and glaring and busting through doors. Not to mention the inexplicable silence. And he stole my knife."

"I see. He's got a personality problem, and yet you celebrated your invitation into our Institution by slaughtering our only gatekeeper."

"Are you still banging on about that?" I asked. "I thought we'd moved on."

"Eorleoch was four hundred eighty-three years old."

"The bones in his moat suggested he wasn't exactly the nicest of gents, so if you're trying to make me feel guilty, it won't work."

"He had four children."

"Stop."

"And a pet rabbit."

I snarled at Aengus. "You should have been more specific about the task if you didn't want me to kill him."

Still in the open air, he was leading me north. Silence hung heavily over the old fortress. We passed by several towers until, at last, Aengus paused under an archway. On either side of the archway's openings, a portcullis was raised partway, giving it the appearance of a gaping mouth with iron teeth.

As Aengus pulled a skeleton key from his pocket, I ran my fingertips over the rough stone walls. "Why do I feel like a prisoner here?" I asked.

"Because you are. If you attempt to escape, we will sever your head with an iron ax."

"Nice."

The door creaked open into a dark stairwell lit by a few candles. Inside, the air was musty. Golden runes glowed on the walls, and while I couldn't read the ancient fae language, I had a feeling that the runes provided a type of magical security. No one would be going in or out of the Tower unnoticed. Still, it was beautiful. Among the runes, honeysuckle grew all over the walls, and the ropes of plants seemed to move and shift like giant snakes.

I followed Aengus up several stories of crooked stairs.

We crossed into a cramped stone hallway. Silvery light streamed in through the windows.

"Hang on." I needed to get my bearings. I peered out the window to my left. From here, I had a view of the Institute's interior. A riot of vibrant wildflowers dappled long grasses beneath us. With this view, I confirmed my theory about the layout—we were standing within one of the U-shaped stone walls surrounding the Tower Green. And in the center of the Tower Green stood a pale, castle-like building with peaked turrets. Blooming flowers twined its ragstone walls. I thought it might be the oldest part of the Institute.

"Come on," said Aengus.

"Just a sec." I crossed to the other side. From that window, I could see the city of London spread out like a sea of twinkling jewels. Twenty-five years ago—when the four Horsemen had roamed the earth—this would have all been darkness. Apocalypse. Anarchy. And now, everything had returned like it once had been—except with the added horror of the spell-slayers.

I'd once read that the Great Fire in 1666 had completely destroyed most of London. The seventeenth century architects had planned to build a new world—one with wide, modern boulevards and straight roads that actually made sense. While they were making their plans, London's residents just went back and built everything the way it was, sticking to the crooked, winding, and completely nonsensical street patterns they'd been using forever. It was the same thing after the Anarchy. Everything just resumed the way it had been before the angelic apocalypse. Same bars, same food, same technology. Even the same brands and shops.

"I won't wait any longer." Aengus had already moved on, and he stood before one of the doors farther down the hallway.

I sighed, crossing to him. When I reached him, he was turning a key in the lock.

"Are you going to tell me what happens next? What our next trial is?" I asked.

"I'm sure Melusine will fill you in." Was that a hint of mockery in his tone? "But you might want to turn off that headlamp if you don't want to wake her."

I wasn't going to give him the satisfaction of asking him what he meant, but I flicked off my headlamp all the same. The door swung open into darkness, and he motioned for me to enter.

I stepped inside the room, sniffing the air. It smelled a bit of flowers, moss—and something like the damp mud of a riverbed.

The door slammed behind me. A stream of moonlight filtered through a slim window onto a figure—someone sitting bolt upright on a bed. I could just about make out feminine curves and long hair.

I dropped my bug-out bag by the door.

A pair of eyes snapped open, but her expression didn't change. "Oh. A roommate," she said. "They said I wouldn't have a roommate. Guess they were wrong. Training begins in the morning. You've got a wrinkled shirt. Recruited from the streets, weren't you? I see rumpled clothes, and I think 'not a volunteer.' I put two and two together. I get it. You were forced into competing here. A rogue. An outlaw. A ne'er-do-well. I'm not judging. But me? I prefer to follow the rules. You can follow the rules and still be a fun person. I like to think that I'm a kidder. You know, really funny."

Oh, gods. So *this* was Melusine.

"The rest are volunteers like me," she went on. "But they're large, muscular men. That's fine. That's their thing. I see muscles, I think strength. My strength is magic. When we get to the trials that require magic, I will be in my element. Personally, I'm here because of my superior intellect—"

It was at that point I mentally calculated the probability of convincing Aengus to give me a new room. I put the chances of him caring about my comfort just slightly above the likelihood of spontaneously combusting in the night but lower than the chances of randomly getting pecked to death by the Tower's ravens.

I decided to just stay where I was. And in any case, she was already telling me things I probably needed to know. Things like—we were supposed to know magic. And that would be a little problem for me, since I didn't know the first thing about magic.

"My mother *wanted* me to leave Maremount," Melusine continued in a matter-of-fact tone. "She said to me, you never found yourself a suitable husband. Not my fault none of the men could see what a good wife I'd be. I can make four kinds of bread. Corn bread, oat bread—"

I cleared my throat. "It's the middle of the night. Why are you sitting up in bed?"

"—and corn-oat bread, and also a second kind of corn bread with slightly more eggs. Did you ask some kind of question?"

"Why are you awake?"

"I have trained my sleep cycles. I can get twelve hours' worth of sleep in one hour. I don't like to waste time. It's like the old saying goes, even the fae will die someday, so you should never sleep."

"That's not a—never mind. I'm just going to go to sleep on the floor, and we'll catch up tomorrow."

"The floor. Interesting. I see floor-sleeping, I see a backpack you don't need—probably full of emergency items you can't part with—I think traumatic history. Ready to flee at any moment. Keep all your stuff with you. Get attached to items and not people if you can help it, keep your stuff close and expect the worst. I put two and two together."

Gods save me.

I couldn't see much in the darkness, just the dark contours of parallel beds and a dresser against the wall.

I pulled off my boots and stumbled over to one of the darkened corners of the room. I curled up on the floor, finding that a lush carpet covered it, soft against my cheeks. It smelled of the earth, of home.

Melusine was still lauding her intellectual powers as I let my eyes shut. Images swam in my mind—of Ciara, tied to the chair, a gag in her mouth.

Despite the horror of what lay within my skull, it turned out, Melusine's monologues were actually very good for drifting off to.

I WOKE with sunlight streaming into the room, and a vague memory of Melusine trying to wake me. I couldn't remember what she'd said exactly, but it was probably something like, *It's morning now. I always get up early, myself, because it's the best time to have an amazing sense of humor and make four kinds of corn bread.*

Normally, I was a light sleeper, but the magical spell Ruadan had slammed me with was still sapping my energy. I sat up, rubbing my eyes, and I got a clear view of my surroundings for the first time.

I hadn't actually been sleeping on a carpet at all. Thick, lush moss covered the floor, and honeysuckle climbed the stone walls. Wildflowers grew from the ceiling—bluebells, yellow wood-sorrel, and lavender orchids. The beds looked as if they'd been hewn from enormous oak trunks, with branches sprouting into the air around them.

The fae had *really* taken over in here since the apocalypse.

I rose, still wearing yesterday's rumpled clothes, and padded over the mossy ground to an archway leading into another room.

I found a bathroom, but one like I'd never seen. A stone tub rose from the floor itself, like a natural feature that had always been there, and hot spring water bubbled in it. Ferns surrounded it, and pearly sunlight poured in through the window. Enormous, gnarled stags' antlers grew from the ceiling, and water trickled into a rocky sink.

But most importantly, in this bathroom, I wouldn't be getting lectures about the joys of a freshly buried scrotum. In the peace and quiet here, I wanted nothing more than to take a warm bath, but I knew I was already late for—whatever I was supposed to be doing this morning. Possibly learning about magic.

Back in the bedroom, a leaded window looked out onto the Tower Green. Morning light washed over a fireplace, carved wooden furniture, and wooden sconces that grew from the walls.

Given all the wood and candles, I could only hope that some of the glowing runes on the wall managed fire safety.

As I scanned the room, I noticed a handwritten note on my bed.

Tried to wake you. Come to the Great Hall. Cailleach Tower.

Yep, I was definitely late. Not a great start. Slovenly, captured in the streets, terminally late: I was definitely well on my way to achieving Baleros's law about getting the enemy to underestimate you.

CHAPTER 8

*M*y stomach rumbled as I pulled my lavender hair into a bun. I could only hope they'd feed us here. In the meantime, I decided to feast on a grape lollipop from my bug-out bag.

I rushed into the hallway, blinking at the bright light that streamed in through diamond-paned windows. Judging by the angle, it was already past seven.

With my backpack slung over my shoulder, I hurried down the stairs, then pushed through the door into the floral Tower Green.

Which one was the Cailleach Tower? It's not like they'd given me a map, and there were towers all over the place. I was pretty sure Cailleach was a fae name, but I'd never learned much of the ancient language.

I scanned the structures before me, referring to my own mental map of the place. The Institute was made of two concentric rings of stone walls—bordered by the river on one side. But embedded in those stone walls were dozens of towers. Cailleach Tower could be any of them.

Even without an actual map, I was lucky enough to have a powerful sense of smell—stronger even than most full-blooded fae. I sniffed the air. Through the floral scents, I picked up a riverbed smell. That was Melusine's scent, I thought.

I tracked it through the bluebells. The scent was leading me to the largest structure—the gleaming white castle within the fortress walls.

When I reached the enormous wooden door at the structure's base, I pushed it hard. It groaned open to reveal a carpet of vibrant moss spanning a long corridor. I followed it until I reached what I could only assume was the Great Hall.

A wooden floor and rough-hewn wood beams supported the ceiling. A long banquet table spanned the hall, and five other novices sat around it. The room smelled of rich food, and my stomach rumbled. As I crossed toward the table, they all stared at me.

It was at this point, I wished I'd forgone the lollipop, and I popped it out of my mouth, certain my lips had been stained bright purple.

Light filtered through tall windows onto the laden banquet table. The rich scent of baked pudding filled the air. My mouth watered.

It didn't take me long to figure out which one was Melusine, considering she was the only other woman in there. At night, I'd only seen a silhouette. In the daylight, I could see that she had blue hair cascading over rich copper skin. She sat on her own, with a few chairs between her and the men.

The other four were fae males, each of them staring at me with a combination of desire and hatred. I was still wearing my crumpled miniskirt from the night before. Contrary to what Aengus had promised, the Institute had *not* provided us with everything we needed. Not to mention the fact that I was pretty sure I stank of Jack Daniels.

The four fae males looked like purebreds, with pointed ears and elongated canines—which they were already baring at me. Of course they were. Most males from the fae realms treated women as servants, and if you weren't from one of the noble classes, you were basically a sex slave.

And yet….

Baleros's fourteenth law of power: Form bonds with unlikely allies.

I didn't think any of the fae males would be eager to ally with me yet—particularly given the fact that they were all snarling at me. But I decided to take control of the situation, anyway.

"I'm Arianna. Fellow novice."

One of the males had vibrant orange hair, wreathed with oak leaves. He'd pinned his black clothing with a golden brooch, shaped like a scythe. His family's emblem, I imagined. He nodded, nearly imperceptibly. "Maddan, Carver of Enemies, son of King Locrinus of the House of the Golden Sickle."

A prince, then.

"Fintan," said one with bluish skin and waves of green hair threaded with seaweed. "Slaughterer of the Feeble, Son of Og, House of Allod."

I knew his kind—they lived in the ocean and ate humans, apart from the livers, for some reason. Apparently, that particular organ was unclean.

Another wore his long, raven hair slicked back, and dark tattoos snaked over his pale skin. I'd mentally labeled him *Goth Fae.*

He narrowed his dark eyes. "Bran, Slayer of Foe, son of Deurbel, House of—"

But the rest of the conversation was cut short by a loud growl from the fourth fae—one whose claws now dug into the table. He was enormous, with shaggy brown hair, a silver breastplate, and a metal helmet shaped with hounds' ears. He wore a tunic of black fur. I had a feeling he was a barguest—a ferocious fae that could transform into a black hound.

His horned metal helmet was nearly falling off his head with his fury, and his fiery eyes were locked on me. I wasn't sure if he hated me for being female, a gutter fae, or if he gave everyone that sort of greeting.

Fine. I didn't really care who his dad was, and I'd just be calling him Dog Boy.

As the barguest's growl died down, a hush fell over the room.

Maddan—the prince—sniffed the air, his lip curling. "You're not a noble Mor, or I'd know of you. No wonder it smells like a gutter fae in here. Female, as well. The knights must be getting desperate."

"A gutter fae," Bran repeated. He sniffed the air, too. Not very creative, this one. "You reek like the bottom of a whiskey bottle."

I cocked my head. "You say that like it's a bad thing."

The barguest growled. "The gutter females in my kingdom are whores. I use them. When I finish, they beg for a coin or two, and I squeeze their throats till they go quiet again."

Change of plan. I was not making alliances with these twats at any point. In fact, I was going to kill Dog Boy. Somehow during these trials, I'd be running a blade through his chest.

"Agreed." Sea Monster narrowed his eyes at me. "Where I come from, women like that are used for sport, and then discarded."

"Where you come from?" I crossed my arms. "A trawler's net, was it?"

"Once," continued Maddan, drumming his fingertips on the table, "only noble males were allowed in the Institutes. Now they've opened their doors to any old gutter whores. It's almost enough to make me reconsider my choice to come here."

I cocked my head. There was only one reason noble males like this came here, and it wasn't exactly by choice. "But you don't have any other options, do you? Your older brother will inherit your father's title, and you're shit out of luck." I leaned on the table, looking him right in the eye. "Now you ask yourself why the knights would allow a gutter fae female outlaw in here. And a demi-fae, at that. One with a shady history like myself. Why would they break with tradition? Maybe, just maybe, it's because they know I'm exceptionally skilled at killing." I nodded at Melusine. "And maybe Melusine over there has some skills of her own. You'd better hope you get the chance to crawl back home in disgrace, but I think your chances of surviving are slim."

All four fae males snarled, baring their canines again. And while they got on with that asinine display, I mentally calculated how I could maim all of them in the next thirty seconds. The barguest would be first— I'd use his own knife in his throat. I'd kick Sea Monster in his head, then throw his knife into his chest. By then, the other two would be reacting. Bran would get a shard of ceramic plate in his neck, and Maddan—I think I'd kick Maddan half to death on the wood floor.

I folded my arms, smiling at the mental image. "Anyhoo, nice to meet you all. I'd better eat before I get cranky."

I crossed to Melusine, who'd ignored the entire encounter. Given that she'd chosen to sit a few seats away from the males, I was starting to give credence to her whole "superior intellect" claims. Best to avoid those arseholes all together.

Now, she was focusing completely on cutting up her food and eating it with remarkable efficiency. If I were going to make any allies here, she seemed like the most reasonable starting point. I dropped my backpack on the floor and pulled out a chair across from her, my mouth watering again at the rich smell of the fae food.

Of all the supernatural creatures, the fae in particular were known for their cooking. Before me lay a plate of strawberries, bread pudding, and apples drizzled with honey.

Maybe being a novice of the Shadow Fae wasn't the worst thing in the world.

Melusine kept her eyes on her food as she ate. "We'll be matched this morning."

"Matched?" I asked.

"Yes. We'll find out which knight will be training us. They're all highly skilled. Obviously, I wouldn't want to be matched with Ruadan."

The buttery bread pudding melted in my mouth. "And why is that?"

"He doesn't speak, which would make training with him difficult, and I heard he killed his last two novices. Snapped their necks. After they fell, he severed their heads with an iron blade."

My stomach clenched. This certainly wasn't getting any better. *Hang in there, Ciara.*

CHAPTER 9

I blinked in surprise. "He's silent and he kills his novices," I murmured. "Those are good reasons to avoid him."

She sliced a strawberry in half. "I told you. Superior intellect."

"Any idea why Ruadan doesn't talk?"

"Vow of silence, I heard. He won't speak until he's killed … someone. He's just really into killing, I think."

"No idea who it is?"

She cocked her head. "Have you heard the rumors that two Horsemen of the apocalypse remain alive? In magical realms. Death and Conquest. I think Ruadan wants to kill them, and their offspring. I mean, everyone knows angels don't belong on earth, and they caused all this. All the wars. The death."

"Oh." A silence fell over us. "I don't think I ever told you my name. I'm Arianna."

"I'm Melusine. I'm not good with people."

"You and me both." I leaned in closer, whispering, "Since you obviously know a lot of stuff about things, what else can you tell me about the Shadow Fae?"

"There are Shadow Fae Institutes all over the world, but this is one of the oldest." Melusine speared her fork into two strawberry slices. "The Grand Master of the London Institute is incredibly powerful. In fact, he controls mist. He has an entire army he can summon from fog, though I've never seen it. He acquired it by slaughtering the last Grand Master. It gets passed on, like an heirloom."

"A mist army. That sounds a bit ominous."

"All the Shadow Fae have a kill list."

"Any idea who's on the list? Besides the Horsemen and the angels?"

"Nope. I expect our mentors will tell us." She looked at my plate, frowning. "You have one less strawberry than everyone else." She speared a strawberry on her plate, then deposited it on mine. Then, she returned to cutting up her strawberries into pieces.

I was beginning to find Melusine oddly endearing. "So, this match you mentioned. How do we—?"

The clacking of heels over the floor cut my sentence short, and I turned to see a fae male stalking into the room. By the mist curling around his body, I knew this was the Grand Master. His white hair was pulled back, and a silver crown gleamed from his head. His clothes were trim and tidy, and he wore a bow and arrow strapped over his back. I wasn't entirely sure how he managed to use the bow, because one of his arms was missing—replaced with a silver replica.

His body glowed with pale light, and I could feel the power he exuded rippling through the room. He wore a silver brooch shaped like a horse pinned to his cloak. But most disconcertingly, in his good hand, he carried what appeared to be a human skull—at least, I thought it was human. It had been fashioned into a sort of drinking cup with silver flourishes, and mist twined around it. He took a sip from it as he prowled over the floor.

Suddenly, I'd lost my interest in the food.

He raised his skull cup into the air. "Novices of the Shadow Fae! I am Grand Master Savus. You have volunteered in the hopes of joining our esteemed ranks." His pale eyes landed on me. "*Most* of you have volunteered. Now, there are those outside these walls who call us spell-slayers. But we do not view our role as killing. We view it as protecting and as sacrificing. Shadow Fae serve the Old Gods. Gods who draw strength from sacrifices. We have always accommodated the gods with fresh blood. We have likewise protected the fae from demonic enemies, and we continue to enforce law and order today by slaying monsters who no longer belong here."

At this point, the six Shadow Fae Knights strode into the room, all of them wearing cloaks in different colors. Aengus wore green, Ruadan wore black, and the rest wore vibrant nature colors, like the orange of turning leaves and the pale blue of a lake under the sky.

C.N. CRAWFORD

Like most high fae nobility, the six males were beautiful.

In the daylight, I could see Ruadan's features better. Sunlight washed over the chiseled planes of his face and stunning golden skin. Dark magic—demon magic—seeped into the air around him. He wasn't just a fae. He was a mongrel, like me. He must have been half demon. Whatever he was, a dark power rippled off him. Even from a distance, I could sense it snaking over my skin in a dangerous caress.

His violet eyes sparkled with cold silver, and when his gaze slid to me, a shiver danced up my neck.

"Here, at the Institute," Savus continued, "some of you will die during your trials. In fact, only one of you will gain a place among us as a knight. The rest of you will be returned from whence you came." His gaze landed on me. "Or executed, naturally."

Someone tapped my shoulder, and I jumped. Maddan—prick that he was—had moved into the chair behind me. "They're going to kill you," he whispered. "When you fail them."

I bit my lip. Apparently, in addition to finding the World Key, I had to actually take the trials seriously, or they'd execute me.

Good thing surviving trials was something I'd grown accustomed to.

"If you do survive to become one of us," Savus continued, "you will perfect the traditions of the Shadow Fae. You will learn the arts of warfare, magic, and espionage. You will learn to draw power from the earth."

Oh, please *tell me that doesn't involve scrotal burying.*

I glanced at the four males, who sat with their chests puffed. They were eating this up. *Desperate* to become knights.

"The mentor and novice relationship is a divine one," the Grand Master continued. "Among the Shadow Fae, it is known as *anathra*, the sacred bond between a teacher and a student."

I swallowed hard. Baleros had been a Knight of the Shadow Fae, and he'd been my teacher in the arena. Considering he'd kept me in a cage, I'm not sure he'd viewed our bond as sacred, but the fucker had certainly got in my head.

Savus's silver arm shone in the morning light. "Novices and their mentors will be doing everything together. You will train together. You will eat together, sleep together. You may travel to other realms together to learn the art of combat."

My ears pricked up at that. *Traveling to other realms. Is that what the World Key unlocked?*

That was exactly the sort of power-mad shit I'd expect from Baleros. He'd thrived during the anarchic years after the apocalypse. He had every incentive to unleash chaos again, and the best way to do that was to unlock the magical realms. Shadow demons, fire demons, storm demons, fae—all would flood the world once more, fighting for supremacy. And Baleros knew how to profit off chaos.

Savus lifted the skull. "You will begin your trials tomorrow. Your mentors should train you, and with any luck, you will survive the first trial." He smiled. "And now, you will be matched with your mentors, and you will form the bond of the *anathra*. Please understand that we do not choose these matches. The Old Gods choose for us."

I looked around the room, scanning the possible mentors. The knights stood rod-straight. For just a moment, Aengus shot me a half-smile. If it weren't for Ruadan and the World Key, I'd be hoping for him right now.

As I stared at the knights, silver magic snaked around the recruits. It brushed over my skin in a cool rush of tingles, raising the hair on the back of my neck. The power felt immense. It smelled of the ancient fae forest—of oaks and moss, lichen and rich, fertile soil—and darker things, like bones and blood. I closed my eyes, breathing in deeply. *Home.*

Across from me, Melusine yelped, and my eyes snapped open. She was clutching her arm, staring at it, wide-eyed. She beamed, looking up. "Aengus!" she read.

His green eyes gleaming, Aengus crossed to her, and he led her out of the room.

I scanned the other knights, my breath quickening. Ruadan's magic whirled around him, darkening his form and making him indistinct. Despite the fact that I needed the World Key from him, I *really* didn't want to spend any more time with him.

I shot a glance at the other recruits, and Maddan leaned closer to me. "You'd better hope you don't get the Wraith. He slaughters his novices."

I simply snarled at him in response. They already viewed me as gutter fae trash, so I didn't see the point in trying to act dignified around them. Let the fuckers underestimate me.

In any case, I *needed* to get paired with the Wraith, even if he had the unfortunate tendency to kill his novices. He had exactly what I wanted.

Bran—the goth one—straightened, lifting up his sleeve. Then, he read the name. "Eifion."

A knight in a crimson cloak lowered his cowl. Olive leaves wreathed his dark hair, and he solemnly crossed to Bran.

The two of them crossed out of the hall, footfalls echoing off the high ceiling.

I breathed in deeply, and a hot pain seared my forearm—like the magic that had branded my neck. I smelled burning skin. I pulled up my sleeve, and my pulse raced. I was both scared and delighted by what I found.

There—tattooed in black on my forearm—was the word *Ruadan.*

I looked up to meet his gaze.

But instead of walking over to me as the others had, he shot me a look of pure disgust.

Then, he turned and stalked out of the room, his shadowy magic trailing behind him.

For Ciara's sake, I needed to be matched with him, but my chest clenched all the same.

The other novices snickered behind me.

"What a shocking surprise," said Maddan. "Even your mentor wants nothing to do with you."

CHAPTER 10

*B*efore running off in search of Ruadan, I returned to the beautiful room I'd shared with Melusine for a hot bath.

Now, I wanted to stay in the warm, bubbling bath forever. It smelled of wildflowers and moss in here. *Home.*

When I sank deeper into the warmth, a vision bloomed in my mind—my dream palace, with the river and the sweet scent of apples. I felt safe there.

Steam curled around me.

Sadly, I was supposed to leave this lovely room. The Old Gods had decided that I should sleep in the same room as a silent assassin who slaughtered his novices, and who was I to argue with gods?

I dried myself off, my gaze roaming over the scars that marred my arms, my abdomen. My chest, too. Basically, my skin was a wreck, but I was proud of it.

Every inch of jagged, raised flesh was proof of my ability to survive. There was a crooked scar below my belly button, where a vampire had stabbed me with a sword. A deep divot by my collarbone where a hellhound had impaled me with a spear. My arms, covered in grooves and ridges from a hundred sword fights. And most importantly—the deep scar on the inside of my right wrist where Baleros had branded me with his symbol. As soon as I'd escaped the arena, I'd cut the brand off.

If I'd been human, many of these wounds would have killed me.

I wrapped the towel around myself and gazed at my face in the steamy mirror. The hot bath had pinkened my cheeks, and the water had slicked my long eyelashes into black peaks. My amber eyes looked bright in the late morning light.

At least my gladiator opponents had left my face unmarked.

I knew a woman was never supposed to admit when she thought she was beautiful. It was a mortal sin. Everyone hates a woman who likes how she looks, and women are especially reviled if they're flawed and still have the balls to feel beautiful. Covered in scars, not the right shape, wrong hair—whatever. You're supposed to feel bad about it. So I just kept my thoughts about it to myself. I was scarred; I was beautiful, and I didn't need to know what anyone else thought about the matter.

Baleros's eighth law of power: Conceal your true intentions.

Considering I had nothing else to wear yet, I'd managed to wash my clothes in the bathtub. Then, I'd hung them out the window to dry in the sun, but they were still damp when I pulled them on. The fabric clung to my skin.

I crossed into the mossy bedroom one last time, already dreading having to hunt down Ruadan.

On the way out the door, I threw my bug-out bag over my shoulder. Ruadan had taken all my knives from me, so if he tried to murder me in my sleep, I'd be at a *slight* disadvantage. But he'd left me with the lighter and aerosolized deodorant. I guess makeshift flamethrowers weren't one of the ancient fae traditions.

As I hurried down the stairs, I wondered who Baleros's "eyes" were in the Institute. And why hadn't he asked them to steal the World Key for him? Why did he need me to do it?

I crossed outside into the bright air. On the lush, wildflower-covered green, I sniffed the air. The scents of bluebells, orchids, and fresh grass overwhelmed me. But layered under those—pine. Ruadan's scent. I started moving, my pulse already racing at the thought of seeing the Wraith again. I tracked his smell across the green, and it grew more powerful as I walked. The sunlight warmed my skin.

At last, the scent of pine led me to a circular tower with thin arrow slits and diamond-paned windows at the top. It stood near a low stone gate that opened to the river. I was pretty sure that long ago, human monarchs had ferried traitors through it, from the Thames into the Tower. Once through the gate, they'd never taste freedom again.

Right now, I felt a strong sense of kinship with those poor souls.

I circled the tower's base until I found a black, studded door, and I pushed through it into a stark stairwell.

As I climbed the winding stairs, I reviewed my mission. I had to stay focused on the World Key, without ever giving away my true intentions. I needed Ruadan to let down his guard around me, which right now seemed like it would be nearly impossible.

How would I earn the trust of the demonic assassin, someone so hell-bent on slaughtering his enemies that he wouldn't speak until he'd achieved the task?

My footsteps echoed off the stone tower walls.

Baleros's tenth law of power: Always think three steps ahead.

Once I'd stolen from the Wraith, what the fuck was my exit strategy?

I didn't have one. Even if I managed to kill Ruadan before I made it out of here, in itself a difficult task, I'd then find myself with the entire Order of Shadow Fae hunting me down to the ends of the earth until they meted out a gruesome death.

At this point, I was deeply regretting having never learned the ancient fae art of glamour. Though maybe even that wouldn't help protect me as a fugitive on the run from the Shadow Fae.

I swallowed hard, following Ruadan's masculine scent down a long, vaulted hallway. Maybe I could steal the World Key without anyone here noticing it was me.

What if I found a way to pin the crime on the prince? Two birds, one stone.

Baleros's eleventh law of power: Use the destruction of your enemies to achieve your own goals.

At last, the scent of pine led me to a door at the end of the hall. I sucked in a deep breath, then knocked. After a moment, Ruadan pulled it open. He glared down at me, silver flashing in his eyes.

For the first time, I saw him without his cloak on. He wore knives strapped to his waist, and a sword on his back. His shirt hugged his body, which looked thickly corded with muscle. I could see a few scars on the exposed skin of his wrists. Every inch of him was a warrior, and I got the sense that he was old. I wondered how many battles he'd fought over the centuries, how many lives he'd taken. It was hard not to feel small and vulnerable as I stood in front of him—a feeling I was not at all accustomed to.

Coldness gleamed in his eyes, and the vicious glare he was giving me slid right through my bones. No wonder the Shadow Fae terrified everyone.

I loosed a breath, trying desperately to ignore the instinct that told me to run away from him as fast as I could. "Looks like we're matched. I can see by the look on your face that you're as thrilled as I am."

That look kept me rooted in place, and I willed my breathing to slow down. I tried to imagine my frantic heart beating a little slower. I had to gain control.

He pulled the door open wider, and I crossed into the room. Ruadan's room was more sparsely decorated than the one I'd slept in last night. A perfect match for his effervescent personality.

There was no moss on this floor—just stark, gray stone. And in here, no flowers grew. Instead, flecks of jet-black rocks gleamed in the stone walls. His bed seemed to rise from the stone floor itself, as if the ancient flagstones had sprouted a resting spot just for him. Likewise, a small stone table seemed to grow from the floor, along with seats surrounding it.

The fae had altered so much of this place with their nature magic. Truthfully, it was all more beautiful than anything I'd ever seen. Even this bleak design.

A bureau stood on one side of the room—and on the other, Ruadan's arsenal hung on the wall: axes, swords, crossbows, knives…. Ruadan had about forty-seven different ways to kill people in here.

I let out a low whistle. "Well, Ruadan, love what you've done with the place. Charming and quaint as fuck."

He simply stared at me. A phantom wind whispered into the room, toying with a lock of his pale blond hair. I felt a pulse of his dark magic ripple over me, rushing over my skin in cold, electric tingles. My back arched at the raw power, pulse racing out of control. I willed myself to calm down again, breathing more slowly, and it took me a moment to compose myself.

I pointed at the bed. "I notice there's only one bed."

His posture was rigid. When I'd first met him, he'd projected a detached disinterest. Now, he stared at me with a sort of disturbing, intense curiosity, like I was an alien species he wanted to eviscerate and study. I couldn't say it was a *warm* look.

Good. I just wanted him to get the hell out of the room, so I could search it from top to bottom. The World Key might be in here. Perhaps I could use his distaste for me to drive him out of here.

I slipped out of my boots, then sauntered over to his bed. I sat on the edge, and I unzipped my bug-out bag. I rifled past matches, candles, and chocolate bars until I found a bottle of Jack buried at the bottom.

Aengus had said I wasn't the sort of recruit Ruadan would like—that he hated slobs, drunks, fuck-ups, bar-brawlers, wastes of space…. Maybe that was the best way to get a little alone time in here.

It was also possible that I was *really* good at finding excuses to justify drinking alcohol.

In any case, I took a sip of bourbon, reveling in the warm tingle down my throat. Then, another, longer sip.

I handed it to Ruadan, wiping the back of my hand across my mouth. "Here. I think maybe you could use some of this. You've obviously got your knickers in a twist about something, and this might help."

Strands of his dark magic lashed the air around him. Then, he pivoted, stalking out of the room.

Beautifully done, Arianna. Let no one say that the ability to piss people off wasn't within my skill set.

And now, I had a World Key to find. I wanted to get Ciara the hell out of that room.

CHAPTER 11

I started with the stark, black bureau. I rolled open the drawers, finding row after row of tidy black and gray clothing. Trousers, sweaters, even underwear. Finding nothing on the first round, I went through it a second time, slipping my fingers into pockets, checking the edges of the drawers. Touching everything, basically. As I worked, adrenaline raced through my blood. I was all too aware of what could happen if Ruadan caught me doing this. The threat of execution hung over me like a … well, like an executioner's sword.

Once I'd completely cleared the bureau, I moved over to Ruadan's bed. It smelled of him, and I found the scent disturbingly pleasing. I pulled down the sheets, slid my hand into the pillowcases. I scoured every inch of that thing before putting it all together exactly as it had been. And at every moment, I was painfully aware that Ruadan could bust into the room.

Or more likely, waft into the room like smoke so that I wouldn't notice him until his hands were around my throat, ready to snap my neck. I worked as quickly as I could.

I wasn't a tidy person, but I knew *how* to clean. It was just that I didn't normally expend the effort, because honestly, who cares? I stepped back, scanning the bed to make sure it looked exactly as it had when I'd come in. Looked perfect to me.

Then, I surveyed the room once more. The only other pieces of furniture in the entire place were the rough stone table and a black desk that stood under one of the windows. But the desk didn't have drawers, just a few blank pieces of paper on top, and a pen.

Still, something about the placement of the desk seemed odd. Everything in this room was so symmetrical, so tidy. But the desk stood unevenly between the two windows—too far to the right.

I crossed to the desk, and I got down on my hands, crawling under it. I craned my neck to look up. Nothing. Then, I scanned the stone beneath the desk. At first, I found only a smooth expanse of flagstone. But after a moment, I noticed something irregular about one of the squares—a smaller square was inset into it.

Now, my pulse was racing wildly. Could this be what I was looking for? I was on my hands and knees under a desk, in a position that had no graceful explanation or exit plan. But I had to find out what he was hiding....

I pried open the small stone, my heart hammering.

But what I found wasn't a key. No, it was a small piece of parchment.

My heart raced out of control as I pulled it out. I sucked in a sharp breath, reading through a list of names—

Adonis

Kratos

They were two of the horsemen—Death and War.

A number of other angelic names ran down the list. Refugees and fugitives from the war decades ago. Then, another name that made my heart leap out of my chest.

Baleros.

I hadn't found his key. I'd found his kill list.

It was about that moment that I became aware of a disturbing feeling of hairs standing on my nape, and goosebumps rising on my skin. I hadn't heard Ruadan come in, but I could feel him looking at me. Generally, I was very good at hearing footfalls and heartbeats, breaths moving closer behind me. But he was the gods-damned Wraith, and he didn't give anything away.

I swallowed hard, painfully aware of how I looked right now. On my hands and knees beneath his desk, in a skirt that was already too short, my pink knickers probably hanging out, and *clearly* reading his kill list. I loosed a long breath, shoving the kill list back into place.

I had a terrible feeling my name would be on there soon.

Then, I slid the stone panel back into position.

With my pulse racing, I backed out from under his desk, my mouth dry. When I turned to look at him, his violet eyes had darkened to pure black.

Oh, *shit.* That was generally the signal that a demon was about to rip your head off.

My knees felt a little weak. "I dropped a coin. It rolled away. Oh well."

Smoky magic carved the air around him, and he shifted in a blur of black to his bed. He lifted his pillowcase, sniffing it. He looked at me, snarling.

Oh, hells. He could smell me all over his bed.

In another blur of black, he was at his dresser, sniffing the air.

At this point, there was really no purpose in denying that I'd searched his entire room. So I started backing up toward the door. "I just wanted to know who I'd be living with. You'd do the same."

My gaze flicked to his arsenal of weapons, but I already knew I couldn't move as fast as he could. He'd be there before I landed my first step. Instead, I continued to back toward the door. His fury spooled out of his body in dark magic, like spirals of ink sliding through water, darkening everything around him. I opened the door behind me, keeping my eyes on him as I stood in his doorway.

When Ruadan growled, my stomach dropped. He lunged for me, picking me up by my ribcage. The next thing I knew, I was landing flat on my arse on the stone floor.

He'd literally thrown me out of his room. *Hard.* Just

a moment later, he hurled my bug-out bag at me, and I raised my arm to block it from hitting me in the head.

"I want my whiskey back!" I yelled as he slammed the door.

He hurled the whiskey bottle at me, and I caught it easily.

And thus began the first day of our beautiful *anathra* relationship.

* * *

SINCE RUADAN HAD THROWN me out of his room, I spent the rest of the afternoon searching the Institute's grounds.

I'd learned that half the rooms were barred by ill-tempered ogres. Granted, I was pretty sure I'd managed to charm one of them—a beer guzzler who'd nicknamed me *Viscountess von Tittington* and kept trying to get me to sit in his lap. I suspected anyone with boobs could charm him, to be honest. Already, he'd told where I could find the Institute's library, and I was now on my way up a hidden spiral staircase, lured by the scent of old books.

At the top of the stairwell, an ancient fae guarded the entrance. Her white hair cascaded down a midnight blue cloak, flecked with stars. A high ceiling arched above us, as tall as a medieval cathedral's. I didn't think this had been here at all when the humans had controlled it, but I loved the addition. Just like the librarian's cloak, it had been decorated with silver stars, moons, and constellations dappling midnight-blue paint.

I peered past the librarian. Glowing balls of light hung in the air, illuminating shelves crammed with ancient tomes. The stacks spanned two stories. Flowering vines grew between the books, and the air smelled of honeysuckle. I could have sworn the vines were moving. Gods, this place was amazing.

The librarian peered at me over the rims of her crescent-shaped glasses. "A novice, are you?" she trilled from behind a wooden podium.

"Yes. Freshly recruited. I'm looking for…." I couldn't exactly come right out and say I was looking for the World Key. "Information about magical realms. I understand the role of the knights is to keep supernaturals in their worlds, using death as a deterrent. And I wanted to read more about the locked worlds."

A whirring sound filled the air as the librarian turned, gliding over the stone floor. It was at this point I realized she was on a sort of wooden Segway with silver wheels, powered by fae magic. It hovered gracefully in the air. Gods-damn, I *really* wanted one of those.

"This way," she chimed.

I followed her into the library, my gaze roaming over the towers of books that reached high up to the vaulted ceiling above us. A flicker of movement in the corner of my eye turned my head, and I caught sight of a large pair of cream-colored moths, fluttering around the books' spines. Their wings looked like ancient paper, and their rapid wing strokes raised dust clouds. Around us, dust motes hung suspended in the air, caught in the light.

"Aren't moths bad for books?"

"Those are the library moths," she said in a tone that suggested I was an idiot. Surely everyone knew about library moths. "They dust the books."

It was at this point, I realized the glowing balls of light were, in fact, giant glowworms. They hung curled up and suspended from the ceiling by thin threads of silk.

This place was a gods-damned orgy of magical knowledge. Magic Segways, towers of books, isolation from other people—I wondered if there was any way I could persuade the Shadow Fae that I should work here instead of becoming a knight. All I asked for in return was the World Key. Killing people was starting to get old, anyway.

She led me to a corner of the library, where pale light shone through steeply peaked windows, breaking through iron-gray clouds. It looked like a storm was about to hit us.

"Here we are," she said. "Magical realms."

The Segway whirred, and she abruptly zoomed up another story. She pulled out a book, blew a cloud of shimmering dust off it. Then, she plunged back down to the ground at an alarming speed, before screeching to a halt an inch above the floor.

Pretty sure my librarian friend had a bit of a risk-taking side. I liked her already.

A flash of light illuminated us. Then, thunder boomed, rumbling over the horizon so loudly it rattled the bookshelves.

Staring at me over the rims of her glasses, she said, "You'll find everything you need to know in there about the magical realms. Maremount, Acidale, Louko-mourie, Lilinor … all of them. It's merely an introductory guide. Once you finish with that" —she waved a hand at the stacks of books— "you can delve deeper with some of the other, more detailed books."

"Can I stay in here as long as I want?"

She shrugged. "Suit yourself." And with that, she zoomed away, her white hair flying behind her.

I sighed. She just might be the coolest person I'd ever met.

I began flipping through the ancient pages, skimming one world after another. The vampire realms, the witch realms, fae realms … none of this was really helping, because none mentioned a World Key.

I paused only at a world labeled Emain—a one-page entry with hardly any information, apart from the words, *Mythical Headquarters of the Shadow Fae.* The top of the page briefly described it as a legendary Shadow Fae world, one that probably didn't exist at all. Apparently, many fae dreamt of it, but no one credible had ever been there.

Still, the pictures had my attention—a palace with columns that overlooked a rocky valley, its slopes dotted with apple trees. I brushed my fingertips over the brittle paper. It looked almost exactly like the palace of my dreams.

* * *

IN THE LIBRARY, I dug into my bug-out bag. I worked my way through chocolate bars, lollipops, and my emergency water supply over several hours. It wasn't like the fae used card catalogues or digital databases, and this was a serious time investment. They just lumped everything vaguely related in one section, and Segway Lady remembered it all.

By the time I actually found something referencing The World Key, night had fallen. The glowworms weren't cutting it in this corner of the library, and I flicked on my headlamp.

I held a large black book in my hand, its spine engraved with the silver words *Protectors of the Realms.* Just the sort of pompous shit that the spell-slayers loved. Sorry—*Knights of the Shadow Fae*.

Unsurprisingly, the book was about them. I half-heartedly scanned the contents, until my blood began to race a little at the sight of the words *World Key.*

I began reading as fast as I could. Apparently, there were six fae Institutes, each populated mostly by noble Mor. Orders of Shadow Fae, Fire Fae, Storm Fae—and so on. Each Order had appointed a *seneschal*—a keeper of the World Key that locked up the magical realms. That, I supposed, was Ruadan. But where did he keep—?

My thought was interrupted by a powerful hand snatching the book out of my grasp.

Crikey.

My mouth went dry, and I looked up into the glacial gaze of Ruadan. Had he seen what I was reading?

CHAPTER 12

I frowned at him. "Gods below. Where did you come from?"

It had fallen so silent I could hear the moths flapping their wings. Shadows darkened the air around him.

"That's right," I said. "You're the Wraith, and you don't speak or engage in the common courtesy of having audible footsteps."

I traced my fingertips over the book spines nearby. Assuming he'd seen what I was reading, I had to find some way to explain it. "Since you didn't seem eager to train me and apparently are fine with leaving me to be executed, I thought I could at least learn about the Institute. I was just learning about the structure and all that, but you snatched my book away. So, are you going to teach me things, or do I have to keep reading?"

He wasn't giving the book back. He just stood there with that unnatural stillness, shadows seeping into the air around him. It's a good thing I had my headlamp on, or the billowing darkness would actually make it hard to see.

"Aren't we supposed to have a magical bond of some kind?" I continued. "Our anathra? I think I may find myself at a disadvantage for tomorrow's trial if I have no idea what it is. Everyone else is preparing for it today. Don't you have any sense of duty?"

He nodded brusquely at the exit, then turned to stalk out of the library. Given his general shittiness with communication, I had to guess that he wanted me to follow him, but I wasn't entirely sure. I could only stare at the two swords on his back as I followed him, wondering if one of them was destined for my throat.

Outside, the thunderstorm had returned, and a loud clap boomed over the Institute. Walking just behind Ruadan, I followed him across the overgrown Tower Green. He paused only to pull the headlamp off my head and toss it into the grass. I picked it up and shoved it back in my bag, then hurried after him. As we walked, the skies opened up, unleashing a torrent of cold rain on us.

I hugged myself, shivering as we walked. Where was he taking me, exactly? I didn't feel great about our little stroll together.

Maybe it was the human history of the place—a Tower Green where monarchs had once burned and decapitated queens, lords, and priests for treason—but I couldn't escape the feeling that he was leading me to my execution. I willed my heart rate to calm, gritting my teeth. I wasn't going down without a fight, and I needed to keep my wits about me.

He led me into a dark passage that cut through one of the ancient tower walls. As we walked through the darkened tunnel, I scanned my surroundings in case I needed a weapon. But I could hardly see anything in here.

Ruadan was more at ease in the darkness than I was, and I wanted to turn my headlamp back on.

"I don't suppose you'll tell me where we're going?"

The response was a glare from cold, violet eyes that pierced the darkness. But in the next moment, the passage opened up into a misty cemetery. All around us, stone graves jutted from the ground at odd angles, like the rotting posts of an old pier.

Fog curled around the graves. As we walked deeper into the cemetery, I read the names on some of the stones.

Lord Aubrey de Vere
Edward Plantagenet, Earl of Warwick
Mark Smeaton
Margaret Pole, Countess of Salisbury
Queen Anne Boleyn

That's where I paused, staring at her ornate headstone, engraved with an elaborate *AB* insignia. It was the first name I recognized, and I knew her story. Beheaded on the Tower Green for the crimes of incest and adultery—or, more accurately, for the heinous crime of continuing to exist after the king had fallen out of love with her.

These were humans who'd been executed here once, long ago. As traitors, they would have been buried in unmarked graves, so I had no idea what this place was.

I wasn't entirely sure what was going on here, but some magic was at work. Perhaps, while the humans had ignored their traitorous dead, the fae had honored them in their own secret burials, in a cemetery cloaked by fae glamour.

I loosed a long breath. It was a place of death, but hopefully not of execution.

"So, what are we doing here?" I asked.

I honestly had no idea why I kept asking him questions.

Ruadan loomed over me. When he reached behind his back to draw a sword, fear raced up my spine. It took me a moment to realize he was handing it to me by the hilt. Razor sharp, its blade gleamed with rain drops.

I gripped it, already feeling more comfortable. As the Amazon Terror, sword fighting had been my particular speciality.

I flexed my fingers on the hilt. "Please tell me this is training for tomorrow and not that we're supposed to fight each other to death right now."

His response was a curt nod.

Okay. Good. We were making beautiful progress in our anathra relationship already.

Lightning cracked the sky above us, illuminating Ruadan's masculine features, tendrils of dark magic, and the rigid set of his jaw. He drew his sword from the sheath at his back. His violet glare cut right through me, and he stood with that eerie, animal stillness—a viper about to strike its prey. The only things moving around him were his hair and his shadow magic.

I gripped my sword, readying my feet into a fighting stance. A gust of wind whipped at my skirt.

Ruadan narrowed his eyes at me, and the ice there slid right through me. In the next moment, he was lunging fast as the lightning cracking the darkness.

My instincts—and training—took over, and I parried. Our swords clashed, and we circled each other, movements fluid like dancers. The only sounds were our feet on the graveyard moss and our blades clanging against each other. A vicious slash from Ruadan, but I pivoted, avoiding his blade. His speed dizzied me, but somehow, it felt as though we could each predict the other's moves. Still, he just kept speeding up, until my breath grew ragged in my lungs. If we kept up this pace, I'd get sloppy.

"Are you training me?" I grunted. "Or trying to kill me?"

He swung for me again, at the speed of a storm wind.

Baleros's sixteenth law of power: Use the element of surprise.

Low to the ground, I slashed for his legs—not aiming to slice them, mind you. I'm not a complete monster. I just wanted to throw him off balance. It didn't work. He leapt up into the air, avoiding my strike. I sprang to my feet again, and the ferocity of our training intensified in a storm of clashing steel and rushing air.

Now I was getting a handle on his speed, and I let my fae side take over as I dodged him and attacked with grace. As we fought, a dark smile curled my lips. My blood sang with the ancient beauty of warfare. It had been a long time since I'd been able to fight anyone who could keep up with me, and my heart thundered in my chest. Rain poured down hard, slicking my hair to my face. Was there anything more perfect than a beautiful fight?

I started driving him back toward one of the monuments. I'd pin him there, point my sword at his throat. Maybe, just maybe, the Amazon Terror was a match for the Wraith.

Dominate. Crush your enemies completely.

Lightning flashed, and when I caught the amused curl of his lips, my stomach lurched.

I'd seen my fair share of combat expressions, and this one read, *I've been fucking with you.*

How was it possible? No one *ever* beat me with a blade. Aengus's warning that my cockiness would be the death of me rang in the back of my skull, irritating me to no end. I gritted my teeth, trying to focus solely on Ruadan. He was driving me backwards, now, cornering me between his sword and the willow tree behind me. Exactly the strategy I'd been trying to use. My blade sparked against his in the darkness, and I took another step back. I was losing ground to him at an alarming rate, but he just moved so breathtakingly fast, so precisely….

I hated losing. I gods-damn hated it.

He fought with a brutal, efficient ferocity that I couldn't match. I'd never faced a man like him in the gladiator ring because a man like him would never let himself get caught in the first place. As I took another step back, a brief flash of self-hatred pierced my chest, so sharp it took my breath away. But in the next moment, it had dissipated.

At last, he had me pinned against the willow tree. With a violent slash, he knocked the sword from my hand. It fell in the dirt, and he thrust the point of his sword at my neck.

Had he just *Balerosed* me? Lulled me into thinking he was weaker and slower than he was so I'd let down my guard? I think he had. And now, he'd pinned me here. I was completely defenseless.

A deep rage roiled in me. I hated being dominated, hated being proven inadequate, and I had to bite down hard on the urge to scream obscenities at him. That wasn't a graceful way to lose. And in any case, I wasn't one to give up so easily. Maybe I wasn't completely defenseless. After all, swords weren't the only tools around us.

Use the environment to your advantage.

Adrenaline snapped through my nerve endings. I channeled my strength, then leapt up, grabbing a tree branch that hung over me. I ignored the sharp sting of Ruadan's blade as it grazed my abdomen, and I gripped the branch. Then, I swung my legs, kicking Ruadan hard in the head. He staggered back.

As I dropped down, he was already bringing the blade of his sword up toward my neck. But I'd anticipated that, and I leaned away from it, thrusting his sword hand away from me. With my free hand, I punched him hard in the chin, using all the force I could muster. Then, I slammed my foot into his gut. When he doubled over, I kicked him in the face again, but he was still gripping his sword.

He straightened. His eyes darkened, and he dropped his sword of his own accord. Somehow, the gesture scared me more than if he'd brandished it at me. Like he'd just been fucking around before, and now he meant business. When he snarled, I had the disturbing feeling that he was about to prove a point—the point being that he could kick my arse without a weapon.

I swung for his face again—but this time, he caught my fist in his hand. Twisting my arm, he whirled me around and slammed me hard into the tree trunk. I didn't give him too much time before I brought my elbow back, hard, into his gut—one, two, three times. He loosened his grip on me.

I dodged around him and started raining punches on him, but he blocked every blow. His arms moved in a blur of speed, and he didn't even look like he was breaking a sweat. The only sign that I'd gotten to him was the terrifying darkness of his eyes, like I was looking into the void itself.

My breath was coming in short gasps, and I was

getting frantic, now. I swung wildly. He ducked. And when he came up again, he punched me brutally hard in the shoulder. A jolt of pain shot through my arm, and I spun from the force, facing the tree.

The next thing I knew, he was gripping my hair with one hand, while his other hand was on my chin, his muscled body pressed against mine. He'd worked me into the perfect angle to snap my neck, and I was completely powerless in his grip. Then, I felt the brush of his canines against my throat. Pure fae domination. I shuddered at the feel of those teeth on my skin. My knees went weak, and I nearly fell.

My pulse raced wildly, my heart slamming against my ribs. I gasped for air. But he wasn't moving, wasn't breaking my spine. I had the feeling he wanted me to cry mercy or something.

I had to remind myself that this was supposed to be training, not a fight to the death. Had I learned something from this exercise? Primarily, not to fight someone known as the Wraith.

"Okay," I gritted out. "You've made your point. You're very strong and manly, and I'm not a match for you. Yet."

Slowly, he released me. I pushed my soaking-wet hair off my face.

Oh, I was in deep, deep over my head with this one.

CHAPTER 13

*I*n the rain, I followed him back to his room in silence. I had no idea what he thought of my prospects in tomorrow's trial. I had to stay alive long enough to find the World Key.

Stay alive, find the key, save Ciara. That was my mission. And after that, I'd have to figure out how to adjust to life as a fugitive. I had a horrible feeling Ciara and I could end up living literally underground again.

By the time we reached Ruadan's room, I was shivering in the drafty castle air. My damp clothing clung to my body. I pulled off my backpack, and my stomach rumbled loudly, practically competing with the thunder. I gripped my belly. "I haven't eaten since breakfast."

Ruadan was doing that thing again where he went completely still and just stared at me, and I was starting to feel just a *little* weird about it.

When I looked down at myself, I realized that the freezing rain had hardened my nipples under my shirt.

That didn't increase my sense of comfort, and I folded my arms in front of my chest. "I'm freezing. I don't suppose you have a bath? And some dry clothes?"

He crossed to the black dresser and opened one of the drawers that I'd rifled through earlier. He pulled out a black tunic—just about ten sizes too large for me—and handed it to me. Then, he nodded at an archway that led into another room. It had no door on it, so ... that was awkward. Then again, Ruadan had so far shown no sexual interest in me whatsoever.

I raised my eyebrows. "I'm going to hazard a guess that when they started this whole anathra thing, only men were involved."

He nodded, and I crossed into the bathroom. Like the rest of his room, the bathroom was sparsely decorated with sleek, dark stone studded with gleaming black rocks. A stone tub jutted from the floor—as if it had grown from it. Steaming spring water bubbled in it.

I peeled off the cold, sodden clothes that stuck to my body. Goosebumps covered my skin, and my teeth chattered.

I stepped into the bubbling water, the heat nearly scalding me, turning my skin pink. Still, it soothed my muscles. Sinking into the bath, I snatched a bar of soap from the side of the tub. I scrubbed my skin, luxuriating in the heat. Then, I soaped up my hair, and dunked my head under to wash it. The soap smelled like lavender. Funny. I hadn't taken Ruadan for a floral soap guy.

I really didn't know anything about him, except that he was a frustratingly skilled fighter, kind of a murdery dick, and obnoxiously beautiful. Oh, and he wanted to kill the man who'd sent me here. From what I'd seen, he had immensely powerful arms—

I clenched my fists, rebuking myself for musing too long about his appearance. I wasn't going to luxuriate here, naked in the man's tub, thinking about his beauty.

I rose, and the water dripped down my skin in warm rivulets. I toweled off, my mind flashing with the disturbing memory of Ruadan's teeth at my throat.

I pulled on his tunic, and it skimmed over my bare skin, reaching to midway down my thighs. My legs had suffered less damage than my torso. I only had a few brutal scars on my right thigh from an irritating dragon shifter who'd briefly pinned me in the arena.

When I crossed back into Ruadan's bedroom, my mouth started watering. On the jagged stone table in the corner of his room sat a warm meat pie, and steam curled from its crust. It smelled of rosemary, potatoes, and steak. *Perfection.*

Fae pies were simply the best thing in the world, and my stomach rumbled loudly again, much to my embarrassment.

I glanced at Ruadan, who still wore his wet clothes. He gestured at the table, and I grinned at the confirmation that it was for me.

Before sitting down, I snatched my bottle of

whiskey out of my backpack and plonked it down on the stone table. I took my seat and drained a glass of water before filling the bottom of the glass with whiskey.

I lifted the bottle to Ruadan. "Care for a dram?"

His violet eyes bored into me.

I took a sip. "Ruadan, your attitude is harshing my mellow."

I cut into my pie. As I ate, I relished every rich mouthful. Whoever had made this had used just the right amount of butter. After six years in Baleros's care, I would never again take food for granted. For every single meal, Baleros had fed us his version of porridge —cold milk mixed with raw oats and a can of beans. Three times a week, we'd get limes so we didn't get scurvy. Nutritionally, it wasn't the worst thing, but it definitely hadn't lit my world on fire.

When I was about halfway through my pie, I glanced over at Ruadan, watching as he peeled off his wet shirt. My eyes roamed over his golden, thickly corded body. Like on me, scars lined his skin. He probably could have healed them if he'd wanted to, but didn't want the unlined skin of a scholar. A single, stark tattoo cut across the center of his back—a rune in the ancient fae language.

When he started to take off his trousers, I quickly focused on my pie again. He obviously wasn't shy about being naked in front of me, and it confirmed for me again that he had no sexual interest in me. I was just one of the guys, an irritating novice warrior he'd been saddled with. But I had functioning eyes and he was stunning, so I couldn't really treat him with the same indifference.

When he'd dressed again, he crossed the room to me, and sat across from me at the stone table. His pale golden hair framed his perfect cheekbones.

My belly was now full, and I leaned back in my chair. "I guess I didn't do so well in our training. Do you have any insight for me?"

He simply shook his head.

I was starting to get frustrated. "That's it? This is how you train someone?"

To my surprise, he reached into his trousers and pulled out a scrap of paper and a pencil. He started writing, the scratching of his pencil filling the silence.

When he finished, he handed me the piece of paper. There, in his looping script, he'd written

You are spoiled and defiant, and a ruthless criminal. You are undisciplined, angry, impulsive, and you fight like a gutter fae.

I snarled at him. "I *am* a gutter fae."

He pointed at the note, and I kept reading.

But you don't need my help for the sword fighting trial. Your skill far exceeds the other novices and some of the knights. Just take care to wipe the smug grin off your face, because it signals when you're about to strike.

"Fair enough."

Then, he pulled my piece of paper from me, writing:

Who trained you?

Conceal your true nature.

I shrugged. "It's just something I've always been good at. Must be in the gutter fae blood."

He narrowed his eyes at me. He clearly didn't believe me, and something like cold fury burned in his gaze. Baleros had once fought with him. How well did they know each other?

I folded up the paper. Since we were actually talking now, in a way, maybe I could bring up the topic of the World Key.

I took a sip of my whiskey. "I've heard some of the trials might happen in different realms. I thought the magical realms were all locked up these days."

He folded his arms. Shadows pooled on the floor around him.

"I know you can communicate now. You just did. You've got an obstinate streak."

He leaned closer, and his cold gaze swept down my body, examining me closely. When his gaze brushed past the thick scars on my thigh, his body tensed.

He shifted, kneeling down in front of me for a closer look at my scar. For some reason, it had piqued his interest. In the next moment, his powerful hands were on my thigh, fingers running over the ridge. I nearly gasped at the unexpected gentleness of his touch.

His brow furrowed. I felt acutely aware of the warm feel of his fingers, his breath warming my skin. He seemed intensely focused on the scar—not in a weird, scar-fetishist way. Just clinically curious. In fact, he was inching up the fabric a little higher for a better look. I tensed, painfully conscious of the fact that I wasn't wearing anything at all under the tunic.

I was starting to get the impression that he had no idea what effect he had on women, which, frustratingly, only made him more attractive. Maybe he was comfortable being naked in front of me, but I wasn't on the same page as him.

His hands inched up just a little higher, and I clamped down hard on them.

He looked startled, as if he'd just been undertaking some kind of scientific investigation and I'd stopped him. Then, he pulled away from me.

I grabbed the edge of the tunic, pulling it down again. I was pretty sure my cheeks had gone bright pink.

He pulled out his pencil and paper again, scrawling.

Where did you get those scars?

"Bar fight," I lied. "Someone threw me through a window after I called him a slack-jawed wank-stain."

Ruadan's expression cleared, as if he should have known all along that I was just an ordinary bar-brawler. He almost looked relieved.

"What happens tomorrow, exactly? Just straightforward sword fighting?"

Another scribble on his paper.

You will travel to another realm. You will fight the other novices, but also demons.

My pulse sped up. *Another realm.* "And how do we get there?" I asked.

His expression shuttered again, and he rose, crossing to his bed. It seemed he knew the World Key was a hot commodity, and if I pushed any harder right now, I risked alienating him completely.

He crawled into his bed and blew into the air. The lights in the candles instantly flickered out, and darkness shrouded the room. How did he do that? That definitely wasn't a fae trick.

Still wearing his tunic, I crossed to a corner of the room and curled up on the floor. The cold stone bit into my bare skin. Okay, so he'd got me a pie, but he wasn't about to stretch as far as giving me a blanket. I understood that he operated with a sort of stark efficiency. He was supposed to keep me alive, and I'd be rubbish in a sword fight if I didn't eat anything. But my physical comfort really had no bearing on the matter, so cold stone was fine for sleeping.

It didn't matter. I was used to sleeping on cold stone, even if I was shivering. In the cage where I'd lived, Ciara and I would tell each other stories every night before bed. Stories about magic, about heroes, about women leading armies to destroy the men who'd oppressed them. Stories about a made-up goddess we called Ciarianna, who slaughtered the grotesque war gods who tried to enslave her. Stories of women who gutted the men who abused them. Lying on the floor, I quietly muttered one of those stories under my breath

—the one about Ciarianna burning a warlord to death. Oddly enough, the gruesome details soothed me.

When I slept, I dreamt of Ciara, sleeping by my side, one arm wrapped around me to keep me from shivering.

CHAPTER 14

*T*he next evening at dusk, we walked out onto the Tower Green. Ruddy sunlight pierced the clouds, staining the sky with hues of violet and amber.

The novices had lined up, with our mentors lingering nearby. We stood on a cobbled square at the apex of a hill.

As soon as we'd arrived at our meeting spot, Melusine had leaned over to me to whisper, "This is where they used to kill people." Given the look of glee on her face, I had the impression that she stopped just short of clapping with delight.

I touched the leather strap on my chest. That morning, Ruadan had presented me with a whole pile of neatly folded clothes: lots of black leather, fitted shirts, and a few dresses. Weirdly, it also included underwear that somehow fit me perfectly, as if he'd taken in my exact measurements. I wasn't sure if he'd picked out the clothing, or someone else. But whoever had selected it had decided I'd look best in sheer black bras and underwear, so that was interesting.

And more importantly, he'd selected one of his own swords for me to use—a longsword of Celtic steel, etched with fae runes.

I glanced at the other novices.

Maddan—he of the golden scythe—sniffed the air when we made eye contact, and his lip curled with disgust.

Evening sunlight glinted off Dog Boy's helmet, and he snarled at me. Why was I supposed to be the disgusting one? The barguest literally turned into an animal who probably licked his own balls, and no one seemed to mind.

Goth Fae was looking straight ahead, the wind toying with his black hair, and the Sea Monster licked his teeth. I swear to the gods I saw droplets of blood on his canines, and I had to wonder if he'd even bothered to leave the liver behind or if he'd just consumed the entire person.

Ravens swooped overhead, cawing mournfully. Even they'd been altered by fae magic. They looked larger than they should be, with glittering black wings. They carried tiny, curled up pieces of parchment in their talons.

Dew dappled the grass, and a heavy mist curled around us.

I glanced at Melusine, who shot me a strained smile. When I looked up and down her body, I could see that she was shaking. Why had they even recruited this poor girl? She must have some hidden skill I didn't know about. It made me more determined to form an alliance with her.

Form bonds with unlikely allies.

As we stood on the cobbles, the mist only thickened further, swirling about us until I could no longer see anyone around me. I heard the sound of footsteps clacking over stone.

"Seneschal." It was Grand Master Savus's voice, and I straightened.

I felt someone brush past me, and I smelled the scent of pine, a flash of pale hair through the mist. Ruadan was their seneschal, the keeper of their keys, and it was probably supposed to be some sort of secret.

I took a tentative step forward, hoping for a better view of the key within all the fog, but Savus's voice stopped me.

"Stay in line, novices."

I froze. This was the closest I'd come to the World Key, as far as I knew. Part of me simply wanted to draw my sword, attack Ruadan, and run off with it. But as he'd demonstrated last night, I wouldn't make it out of that encounter alive.

"Novices!" Savus's voice penetrated the mist. "You are about to enter another realm, one where nothing protects you but your own skill. Some of you may not make it out alive. Your task is to kill as many demons as you can. These demons have been given to us as sacrificial gifts from the shadow realm. They are prisoners in this world." He paused before uttering the final words of his warning. "Because they were too deviant even for demonkind."

A burst of cold magic rippled over my skin, surging through my blood. My back arched at the power. Then, the mist began to thin. When it retreated fully, I found that we were still standing on the Tower Green. Except, this time, it looked like the Tower Green of old. Vines and wildflowers no longer covered the walls. Where the cobbled square had been a few minutes ago, now stood a forbidding wooden scaffold—an execution site.

I glanced at the other novices. Each of them had already drawn their swords, and they scanned the green. An eerie silence hung over us like a funeral pall. If I was going to survive the execution block, I'd have to outcompete the other novices. I had to kill as many demons as possible.

Just as soon as I could find them. Black studded doors blocked most of the entrances to the towers. Were there demons lurking behind them?

I sniffed the air, scenting something unfamiliar. Not fae, no. It smelled cold and musty, like the bottom of a grave. That was where I needed to go.

I glanced at the other novices, who were still hanging around the cobbled area.

At least, until the barguest unleashed a wild, bestial roar, charging for one of the towers. As he did, a white-horned demon burst through a door, dressed in silver armor. I watched as the barguest fought him with brutal swings of his sword. I took just a moment to analyze his form. He had a powerful swing, capable of slicing through a tree trunk, but his technique was a little uncontrolled, and he kept leaving himself open on the right side.

Still, sloppy or not, he was about to slaughter the demon, which meant he was one demon closer to winning than I was.

I sniffed the air again, catching the grave-like scent. I unsheathed my sword, following the smell across the green to one of the towers. I broke into a sprint before any of the other novices caught on that I had a lead.

I kicked through the wooden door into a stairwell, then crept inside, my sword raised. In here, the scent of rot grew stronger, and I followed it up the narrow stairs. Halfway up the tower, the stairwell opened into a great hall—one filled with around a dozen people dressed in gem-studded costumes. A banquet table spanned one side. A melodious song floated in the air.

My jaw dropped. This wasn't the slaughter-fest I'd expected. No, this was a lavish Tudor ball, and the guests wore beautiful masks: swans, butterflies, flowers…. Between balconies above us, vibrant silk swathes spanned the ceiling, flecked with pearls and gems. Jeweled fabric lined the walls, too.

If I didn't have demon killing on the agenda right now, I'd drop my sword and start digging into the meat and potatoes laid out on the table. The Tudors were damned good at throwing parties.

But who, exactly, was I supposed to fight? They didn't even look like demons.

As I stalked into the room, the chatter died down, quiet enough that I could hear my own footsteps and the clashing of swords outside. A roar from the barguest outside pierced the windows. Everyone stared at me.

As the crowd parted for me, a new figure emerged. There, at the other end of the hall, a woman glided toward me. She wore a green silk dress, studded with pearls, and her black hair had been pulled back tightly into a cap. On top of her cap sat a demure silver crown. Was she a queen?

Something about her dark eyes was particularly alluring, and her delicately curved figure gave the impression that she was about to burst out of her gown. She wore a beautiful pearl necklace around her delicate throat. The only thing a bit off about her was the sixth finger on her right hand. Still, my body tingled at the sight of her. In fact, I wanted to touch her.

So *she* was the demon.

An evil queen, perhaps. A warped, demonic, witchy version of Anne Boleyn?

She lifted a graceful hand. "Have you come to join us?" Her voice sounded alluring, an invitation I couldn't resist. I gripped my sword harder. I couldn't bring myself to just swing for her. For one thing, she hadn't attacked, and for another, she was giving me a seductive pout. I kind of wanted to be her friend or give her a hug or something….

I swallowed hard. "I'm looking for a demon."

Her lip curved in a graceful smile, and her eyelashes fluttered. "A demon?" she trilled.

Around her, the small crowd burst into delicate laughter.

Okay, this was really not going as planned. I'd frankly be *much* more comfortable if I'd busted into a room of naked men hacking into each other with swords. That probably said something disturbing about me, but it wasn't the time to dwell on personal flaws.

The witch glided closer again, her body undulating with seductive grace. The faintest hints of dark magic curled around her. A succubus?

My eyes flicked around the room, and I started to think that everyone in here was in her thrall, lured in by her spell. She was drawing me in, too, and I had to resist her.

I lifted my sword, ready to strike, except I couldn't quite bring myself to do it. I needed a different demon to slaughter.

As I stared at her, the woman's ears lengthened into those of a doe, her dark eyes widening. "Touch me not," she whispered, a delicate hand reaching for me.

I could almost hear her heart beating from here, and I was torn by competing impulses to hug her and kill her.

Then, she broke into a run through the hall—but it

only lasted a moment before an arrow pierced her neck. One of the revelers had shot her—a bearded man in a ruff with a sort of beret on his head. His eyes sparked with wild flames.

I gritted my teeth. *He* had a weapon. He had demon eyes. He could die. He nocked an arrow, aiming it now at me, and he fired. I managed to deflect the arrow with my sword.

Definitely okay with killing him. While he was trying to nock another arrow, I lunged for him. I carved through his bow with my sword, then drove it through his chest. Bellows erupted around me. Now, flames gleamed in all the guests' eyes. I was starting to realize I'd misinterpreted the whole situation when I'd first arrived.

I was in a hell world of some kind, and the seductive woman was their victim. Because of course she was—that was how the world worked. Ciarianna would not put up with that shit.

I pivoted, ready to take on the next demon. But at the sound of swords being drawn from their sheaths, adrenaline blazed through my nerves. I'd apparently taken on a crowd of eleven men. I sheathed my sword, a hint of panic whispering in my skull.

Baleros's twelfth law of power: Know when you're outnumbered.

CHAPTER 15

*J*leapt into the air, snatching one of the swathes of fabric. I climbed up, hand over hand, until I reached the mezzanine level, and I swung into one of the balconies. I scanned my surroundings, my gaze quickly landing on a stairwell. I could make a fast exit, but I needed to take out as many as possible on the way out.

My gaze flicked over the lanterns burning brightly in the balcony. Maybe a little fire would help direct things my way.

Baleros's fifteenth law of power: Always use your surroundings.

My pulse racing, I pulled one of the lanterns off its mount and hurled it down to the lower level. The oil ignited, causing a small explosion that lit the fabric on the walls.

I sprinted for the stairwell, then thundered down the stairs, my sword drawn. As the demonic guests began to run for the exit, fleeing the smoke and flames, I drove my sword into them, one by one. In their panic, none of them were prepared for me, and I hacked into them, slaughtering the first two down the stairs. The rest turned and ran back into the burning building.

Smoke filled the air, now, and I turned to flee the tower before the whole thing burned down. When I reached the lower level, the silver-crowned queen raced past me. My jaw dropped. She'd come to life again.

It seemed she'd been condemned to a hell world where she was fated to die over and over again. What crime had she committed? Seduction, probably. In worlds ruled by men, that in itself was some kind of unforgivable witchcraft.

I was dimly aware of the other novices fighting demons around me, but my attention was on the queen, who stood in the grass. Blood spattered her green gown.

From behind her, a hulking, beastly demon burst through one of the iron-studded doors. His body was that of a giant man, bedecked in the robes and furs of a king, and his eyes glistened like white pearls. But his face was leonine, and he had a mane of ginger hair. A golden crown gleamed on top of his head. So, she was the queen, and here we had our king.

My pulse raced at the sight of him, and part of my brain screamed that I needed to run, fast.

I stared as he flicked his wrist, severing the woman's head from her body.

Another demon I'll happily slaughter.

As I ran for him, my sword drawn, he unsheathed his own longsword. He roared, and our blades clashed, steel against steel. His strikes held an immense power, and I struggled to keep my balance.

He roared again, and a powerful blow crashed into my sword. I stumbled for a moment, losing my footing, and he lunged for me, swinging wildly. Regaining my composure, I nimbly dodged back, but he caught me with the tip of his sword, drawing blood from my abdomen. I gripped my gut, my heart thundering.

Oh, shit. I was losing control of this situation.

He slashed for me again, and I dodged. This time, he just nicked me in the hip. A hot stab of pain shot through me.

I clenched my jaw. I needed to get control here.

I gripped my sword hard, striking for him. He parried, again and again, but his size also slowed him down. Now, a familiar strength and surety coursed through me. I knew exactly how to angle my blade, exactly where each step should fall, until I was driving him back into a wall. Power—my legacy, my heritage—suffused my limbs. Still, I took care to wipe the smug look off my face, just as Ruadan had instructed.

I could see that my opponent's form was growing sloppier the longer it went on. I suppressed a smile as he retreated toward one of the tower walls. I *really* liked defeating enemies who were much larger than I was. There was just something about the look of disbelief on their faces….

When he stumbled, I seized the moment and lunged for him, thrusting my sword into his heart. His milky eyes widened in horror, and I pulled out my glistening, red blade.

I'd been injured—pretty badly—but my gladiator training had conditioned me to survive a fight by blocking out pain. Adrenaline raced through me, numbing the agony I should have felt.

Once I slaughtered him, a loud bell began to toll, and a roaring noise rumbled off the stone walls. Streams of demons began bursting through the black wooden doors, racing onto the green, swords and axes raised. They wore jeweled clothing and velvet caps, and many had black wings and talons. My stomach dropped at the sight of them.

It seemed that killing the demon-king in this world was a bit of a faux-pas. In fact, the demons were all bellowing something that sounded like *treason, treason, treason!*

Just as I was contemplating the logistics of fighting off an entire horde of Tudor-era demons, a small whirlpool of water bloomed by the cobbled square.

That was our exit out of here. Already, Maddan and the barguest were abandoning their posts, leaping into the water. Not the *worst* idea in the world. Clearly, the knights had been watching us, deciding when they needed to intervene.

My gaze darted, and I caught a glimpse of a crowd of demons closing in on Goth Fae—Bran, his name was. So much for being a Slayer of Foes. I winced at the sight of his body getting hacked by brutal Tudor swords. He fell to the ground, and his blood stained the grass.

But before I abandoned ship completely, I surveyed the battleground until my gaze landed on Melusine. Two rangy demons in lacy ruffs were boxing her in. I couldn't let them just slaughter her. I raced for them, sword drawn.

As soon as I reached them, I carved my sword into the first demon, slicing through his gut. Then, I whirled, cutting my blade through the other's neck. Blood arced through the air.

"Get to the portal!" I shouted.

I glanced back at the woman in the green dress, who'd come to life again—reunited with her head. Gods-damn it. I couldn't just leave her here, either.

I had just one more task before I left this realm....

Danger was closing in around me, and my canines began lengthening as my fae form took over. Still, I ran for the woman in the green dress, moving as fast as a hurricane, dodging my demonic attackers. Pure power imbued my limbs.

When I reached her, I grabbed her arm. She was shrieking, hysterical, but I dragged her along with me. I used my free arm to fend off attackers with my sword. We reached the portal, and I shoved her into the whirlpool, pivoting one last time to drive my sword into a demon.

Then, I leapt into the portal, and the icy water enveloped me.

The portal sucked me in deeper, drawing me further under. I brushed past the queen's silky dress, and I wrapped an arm around her so I could drag her out with me when the time came. I wasn't sure exactly why, but apparently I'd made it my job to be her protector, and she was coming back to my world with me.

As we sank deeper into the portal, my lungs began to burn, until at last I felt the downward tug relenting. I kicked my legs to bring us up swiftly to the surface. Light began to pierce the water, growing brighter until we breached the surface. I hoisted myself over the stone lip of the portal. Then, I dragged the queen out.

I hauled both our arses out of the water, soaking wet.

On my knees, I struggled to catch my breath. From the ground, I looked up into the face of Grand Master Savus. He looked perplexed, his silver eyebrows furrowed. A splashing noise behind me turned my head. A velvet-capped, black-winged demon was trying to hoist himself from the portal. Instinctively, I swung for him, severing his head from his body. His blood stained the portal red.

As all the adrenaline left my veins, pain slammed into me, and I felt the deep gashes that had been carved into my hip and my abdomen. I realized that my blood was pouring down my body, mingling with the water.

Grand Master Savus cocked his head. "You're a demi-fae. What is your other half?"

I swallowed hard. I'd been hoping that wouldn't

come up, but he must have realized that my strength exceeded that of even a noble, full-blooded fae. "I don't know," I lied. "I was an orphan."

With a swirl of dark magic, the portal began closing up in front of us.

Grand Master Savus glared at the queen, who was sobbing hysterically on the cobbles. "You brought something back with you."

I gripped my stomach, trying to block out the pain tearing through my side. "Sorry about that. She didn't belong there. Those demons were twats."

Swirls of mist poured off Savus, skimming over my skin like some kind of warning. "Well, you successfully slaughtered more demons than any other novice, so I will grant you a bit of leeway."

Melusine crossed to me, grabbing my elbow to help me up. "Why did you kill the demons surrounding me? The other novices are trying to thin the competition, and you decided to keep me in it."

I grimaced, holding my waist. "You gave me a strawberry. Also, we have a greater chance of lasting if we work together."

She nodded. "Oh. I see. It's strategic. I'm not good with a sword, but I can be useful, too."

I believed her.

The three other novices stood on the cobbles, bodies dripping with water. The goth had been killed, but the other males remained. I narrowed my eyes at them.

One down, three to go.

It took me a minute to pick out Ruadan, but he was there, standing behind the recruits. Shadowy magic cloaked him.

But from within his cloud of dark magic, his violet eyes burned with curiosity. I hadn't just surprised the other recruits. I'd surprised him, too.

CHAPTER 16

J sat on the cold floor of Ruadan's room, holding my side. I'd tried to stitch myself up a little bit. Since I didn't know any magic, I couldn't heal myself the way the other recruits would.

In the gladiator ring, the masters had allowed some types of magic—fireballs, electrical pulses, anything that didn't require words. For the most part, gladiators were suspicious of anything that involved language. They liked pointy things and magic that went boom, but they weren't exactly the thinking types.

I sighed. It was probably for the best that way. Someone like me probably shouldn't have access to powerful magic, because gods knew what I'd do with it.

So instead of using magic to heal myself, I'd spent the last twenty minutes gritting my teeth and stitching my skin together with a needle and thread—something I'd done many times before. Sadly, I had to use up some of my whiskey to clean the wounds on my belly and my hip.

The wounds still didn't feel quite right, though, and I only had to hope that the next trial would involve a bit less slicing.

Grimacing, I pierced the final piece of skin with the needle, then tied off the thread. I cut it and collapsed against Ruadan's rocky bed.

Exhaustion ate at me, and I was trembling a little from the pain. Just as my eyes were drifting closed, the door creaked open.

Ruadan glided into the room. His very presence seemed to darken the space around him, the air frosting about us, candles flickering in their sconces.

I shuddered at the sight of him, until he pulled down his dark cowl. Then, my gaze roamed over the stark perfection of his face. The irritating bastard had a way of mesmerizing me.

Given that the gods had blessed him with such overwhelming beauty, it was a shame he always cloaked it with his hood and dark magic. But of course, a man like Ruadan wasn't the type to indulge in trivial things like enjoying life at all.

Aengus pushed through the door behind him, and it creaked on its hinges.

"Where have you two been?" I asked.

Aengus's lips curled in a wry smile. "Trying to figure out what to do with the queen you brought into our fortress."

"Who is she?" I asked, still gripping my side.

Aengus shrugged. "Calls herself Nan Bullen. She's a bit of a diva."

"She's pretty," I pointed out. "Maybe she'll make a charming wife for one of the knights."

Aengus arched an eyebrow. "Has no one told you? Knights of the Shadow Fae are not allowed to take wives. Or lovers. Or anything enjoyable."

I glanced at Ruadan, who'd taken one of his knives off the wall to sharpen it. "I can see why Ruadan fits in so well here, then. He hates fun. He's happiest brooding in his room, sharpening his blades. He takes brooding breaks just to scowl at a bottle of whiskey and glare at anyone with the audacity to smile."

"I hadn't expected you to get to know him so quickly." Aengus frowned at a bra I'd hung from the doorknob, then picked it up by the strap with one finger. "I like what you've done with his room. I'm sure Ruadan loves the feminine touch."

Now that he mentioned it, I realized I'd left items of clothing strewn all over the place. My brain seemed to edit out my own mess until someone pointed it out to me.

"Doorknobs are made for hanging bras," I countered. "It's one of their important functions. Anyway, how is Melusine doing?"

"Alive, thanks to you." He frowned. "Why did you stop to save the queen?"

I shrugged. "Because unpredictability is an asset."

Aengus nodded slowly, his green eyes glimmering,

but I had the sense that he didn't believe me. "And Melusine? Why did you save her?"

"She gave me a strawberry." I surprised myself with the truth.

I guess I *did* like her. I almost groaned at the realization that Baleros knew everything about me. Anyone showing me a tiny scrap of kindness would win my undying loyalty. He knew I'd been desperate for friendship in my cage, that the ruthless Amazon Terror lapped up kindness like a kitten drinking milk. Some sweets tossed on the floor every now and then, and he'd earned my devotion.

I'd escaped the cage, but I wasn't sure I'd ever escape him. I was his slave, even now.

The horror of my realization washed over me. Baleros didn't just think three steps ahead. He thought three hundred steps ahead. Years ago, when he'd noticed my tendency to become attached, he'd given me Ciara. Not because he wanted me to be comfortable —but because he could use her someday as leverage. Like he was doing now. Ciara was just a pawn to him, and always had been.

I shook with anger.

"Are you okay?" asked Aengus.

Ruadan, too, had paused his knife sharpening to stare at me.

"Fine," I said through gritted teeth.

All this only proved Baleros's first—and most important—law of power: *Get in your enemy's head. Knowing someone well gives you power over them.*

Breathe in, breathe out. "Where is Melusine? How is she?"

"Sword fighting isn't her strength, really, but magic is."

I traced my fingertips over my waist. "I was worried about that. Magic. We don't need to know it by any chance, do we?"

Ruadan looked up, raising his eyebrows.

"I can't really do it," I said. "I don't suppose we have a magic-based trial coming up?"

Aengus's features darkened. "Let's just say you two had better start training, then."

My stomach tightened. "I can't just kill things with swords?"

Aengus and Ruadan both shook their heads simultaneously.

"All fae have magic," said Aengus. "You just have to learn how to channel it. Not to mention whatever your other half is."

Oh, friend, you do not want me to unleash my other half. I loosed a long, slow breath. "Fae nobility train with magic from the age of four. How am I supposed to compete with that?"

Aengus shrugged. "You just have to survive." He nodded at Ruadan. "He's half-demon. None of us knows what your other half is, exactly. But the combination of fae and something else can be powerful, just like it is for Ruadan. His magic is more powerful than that of any knight here, including the Grand Master's. You couldn't have been matched with a better person

129

to train you. You see? The Old Gods know what they're doing."

"Except that Ruadan hates me and he can't explain things to me in words."

Ruadan folded his arms, leaning back to glare at me.

"You are talking about him like he's not here," said Aengus. "He's silent, not deaf."

"Right. Sorry."

"And he doesn't hate you. He just doesn't … respect you."

"That's lovely. Cheers."

"Because of the alcohol, and the bar-brawling, and general pointlessness of your existence, and—"

I held up a hand. "Yeah, we've been over it. He wrote it down for me. It was pretty much the one thing he wanted to communicate." I frowned. "So why did you both choose me to come here?"

Aengus shrugged. "Because of how you fight. That's it. You're fast, clever, and ruthless. We could tell that before you even stabbed me in the neck. And we were right to choose you, because no novice before managed to slaughter the King of Mammon." Aengus rubbed at his throat, as if remembering the pain I'd caused him. "Anyway, I have to get back to Melusine. Good luck with your magical learning."

Tendrils of dark magic slid through the air around Ruadan. He stared at me, still sharpening his knife. Aengus wasn't kidding that his magic was strong. It was coiling over my skin right now, raising my hair and making my back arch. A memory burned in my mind—his hand gripping my hair, his teeth on my throat.

The combination of his knife-sharpening and coils of magic was deeply unsettling. I tried not to think about the fact that he'd snapped the necks of his last two novices. I never wanted to be on his bad side.

Too bad I didn't have a choice.

Cold dread spread through my veins. When I'd brought up the World Key before, he'd closed off. He didn't trust me one bit, which was a problem. Ruadan wasn't going to let down his guard at all around me.

I hugged my side, wincing a little. "Can we get some sleep now? It's been a long day, and I need this to heal."

Ruadan frowned, dropping his knife onto the stone table. Then, he rose, crossing to me.

He extended a hand to me, and surprise sparked in my chest. An unexpectedly friendly gesture. I took his hand and rose, and he walked me over to his bed. Then he gestured for me to sit down. I sat on the edge of his bed. The mattress was firm and unforgiving, because it was Ruadan's, and of course it was.

To my increasing surprise, he knelt before me.

Things did not get any less surprising when he began to pull up my shirt.

"Whoa!" I stopped him, tugging on the hem. "What are you doing?"

He cut me a sharp look. I'd irritated him again. Wasn't hard to do.

He pulled another small piece of paper and a pencil

C.N. CRAWFORD

out of his trousers, and he started writing again. Then, he thrust the paper at me.

You need to heal.

"That's where sleep comes in."

He shook his head.

"You have healing powers, I suppose." Given all the shadows and darkness that whirled around him, it wasn't surprising. Shadow demons were known for their healing skills. Demons of death, demons of sleep, demons of easing the pain. They were like the opiates of the demon world, addictive and lethal at the same time.

I didn't want him to see the scars that slashed across my body—my hips, my belly, really every part of me that I'd covered up. Then, I could no longer pass off the lie about the bar fights. Once he saw my scars, he'd know that I'd been a slave, one forced to fight.

If he thought I was ruthless just because I'd stabbed Aengus in the neck, he'd have a whole new definition of the word once he understood I was the Amazon Terror. That I'd slaughtered thousands to survive. Only the most brutal killers survived the arena.

And more—he'd know the worst thing about me: that I was the sort of sloppy, careless person who'd allowed myself to be captured in the first place. That I'd allowed someone to control me for years. Knowledge was power, and I didn't need Ruadan learning that much about me.

My stomach clenched, and I shook my head. "No," I said quietly.

I didn't know why, but I felt tears stinging my eyes as I stood up. For some insane reason, I really wanted his approval. Why? I didn't even like him, but I already yearned for his respect. Possibly because I knew I'd never get it.

I lay down on the cold stone floor and curled up, ready to sleep. The stone chilled my skin, and I shivered.

Ruadan crossed to his bed, and he blew into the air. Darkness blanketed the room.

As I closed my eyes, loneliness carved through me, so sharp it blocked out the pain of my wounds.

he next day, The Wraith and I stood at the perimeter of a stone hall. Through thin arrow slits in the walls, light blazed, illuminating Ruadan's smoky magic. Given our slight communication difficulties, I wasn't entirely clear what sort of magic we'd be practicing today. I only hoped it didn't involve memorizing Angelic spells, because that wasn't my strong suit. And I *definitely* didn't want to have shamanic sexual relations with a potted plant, if that was on the agenda.

I dropped my backpack on the floor. I'd brought my whiskey with me just in case I needed a bit of Dutch courage, but I'd try to keep it capped.

Ruadan wasn't wearing his cloak today—just fitted, dark, woolen clothes that sculpted his body.

As I stood against the wall, he crossed into the center of the room, his back to me. My body tingled, heart racing as his magic thrummed through the room.

I breathed in deeply as it pulsed through me in powerful waves.

As he worked his magic, he touched something around his neck. My pulse quickened. Was that the World Key?

I inched closer, silently. And yet even with my stealth, his body tensed. He flung up a hand, a signal to stop me from moving any closer. He still mistrusted me, and I had the disturbing sense that he could always predict my actions.

Frustration rippled through me, and my fingers clenched into fists. I was getting nowhere here. Ruadan had what I needed, but he wasn't letting me get anywhere near it.

Sometimes, when killing wasn't the answer, I was all out of ideas. But an impulsive attack wouldn't get me very far. He was too clever and too powerful to overcome. I needed to earn his trust, even if it killed me.

As shadows lashed the air around him, his powerful magic intensified, stroking my limbs like a brush of velvet. It heated my skin.

For a warrior who hated to enjoy himself, he sure could work a disturbingly pleasurable spell.

I stared as he unlocked a world, and a pool of water formed in the floor. It spiraled larger and larger until it formed a portal, at least six feet across. I backed away from it, suddenly a little nervous. I wasn't a huge fan of the unexpected unless I had a sword in my hands, and right now I just had my backpack of lollipops and duct tape.

Ruadan gestured for me to move away from the portal, and anticipation hung over the room.

As I took a step back, I stared at Ruadan's throat, searching for something that looked like a key. I couldn't see anything—not a necklace, nor a brooch. Where in the seven hells was he hiding it?

A splashing in the water interrupted my thoughts. Then, an enormous man hoisted himself out of the portal. No, not a man—a demon. One with leathery black wings that swooped down his back and tattoos that were whorled over his chiseled body and olive skin.

I wasn't sure what was more disturbing: the fact that he'd just crawled out of a portal in the stone floor, or the fact that he was stark naked. Like Ruadan, he seemed to think his nudity was unremarkable. He just stood before us with the water from the portal dripping down his powerful body, like *not a big deal, just crawled from another realm with my penis on display.*

His eyes were deep gray-blue, and I tried to focus on them, even if my gaze kept drifting downward as if of its own accord. It took me a moment to realize he was gripping something in his hand.

And another moment to realize he was just sort of staring at me, his brow furrowed. And that we had been standing like that for an awkwardly long time, part of which had involved me staring at his penis.

I cleared my throat. "I have no idea what I'm supposed to do now."

For a moment, only the dripping of water filled the silence.

Then, I nodded at Ruadan. "He doesn't talk. Please tell me that you do, or this will just stay really awkward. I mean, more than it already is."

"I'm Bael, Sword of Nyxobas of the Shadow Realm. Ruadan never mentioned you were a woman."

"I am, yes. He didn't mention that you'd be naked. Mentioning things isn't really his forte, as it happens."

Ruadan shot me a sharp look, his violet eyes sparking with silver. He was part shadow demon. Was he related to Bael?

"The Institute never recruited females in the past," said Bael.

I folded my arms. "Will this be a problem for you?"

"No." He nodded at Ruadan. "My old friend, here, has asked me to instruct you in our ways."

"In the ways of the shadow demons?" I bit my lip. "I guess your ways don't involve trousers."

"I will not sully the waters of Nyxobas, God of Night."

Sure, and I guess he doesn't mind your balls all over the place.

All I knew right now was that the demon standing before me exuded powerful magic that snaked off his body, mingling with Ruadan's. With the two of them in the same room, the power almost overwhelmed me.

On top of that, the room had become freezing with shadow magic, and frost iced the stones.

Given that it was summer, I was wearing nothing but a short dress Ruadan had given me—black, cotton, with frankly more cleavage than I normally showed. But here, in a room suffused with powerful shadow magic, goosebumps rose on my skin, and my teeth began chattering.

I hugged myself. Right now, I was working really hard to keep my gaze on his eyes. "Okay. So what are we doing here?"

"The Institute of the Shadow Fae is tasked with keeping shadow demons in line. They are the fae ambassadors to our demon realm—the shadow realm."

"Okay, I'm with you. What's the next trial?"

"First, a little background. Centuries ago," he continued, "the God of Night exiled the incubi from his realm. All except his son. The God of Night loathes pleasure and the vices of the body, while the incubi feed off pleasure."

"He sounds like a good time," I said. "He and Ruadan would have the best parties."

A heavy hush fell over the room, so heavy I could hear my own heartbeat. Ruadan cut me a death stare, his violet eyes darkening. Clearly, I'd said something wrong.

"Moving swiftly on…" I prompted.

Bael straightened. "The Shadow Fae have been hunting exiled incubi for centuries. The incubi breed heavily, and their numbers keep growing. And now, a nest of incubi have turned up in East London. Your next trial—along with the other novices—will involve hunting the incubi. You need to send them to the shadow hell."

Hunting. I liked the sound of that. It sounded like I'd be able to use weapons. "And we need magic for that? Why not just use swords? Or arrows? Or broken bottles or whatever?"

Bael stared at me for a moment before answering. "You will use your sword. But the incubi are experts in shadow-leaping. That is the magical skill you must learn."

Interesting. "What's that, exactly?"

Instead of answering, Bael disappeared in a blur of dark magic, leaving behind only wisps of dark smoke. It took me a moment to realize that he'd reappeared behind me. Still naked as hell.

"That is shadow-leaping," he said. "Moving from one shadow to another."

I'd seen Ruadan do that. I'd never seen anyone in the arena who could shadow-leap. It brought me back to a previous thought that raked at my mind: a warrior who could shadow-leap never would have been enslaved by Baleros. I *wanted* this skill.

My jaw dropped. "You really think I can learn that?"

He lifted a pendant in his hand—a rock that glowed with stunning violet light. In fact, the color wasn't altogether different from the violet of Ruadan's eyes.

Bael handed it to me. "I've brought you a lumen crystal from the Shadow Realm. Put it on, and Ruadan will teach you how to absorb the magic so that you can use it to shadow-jump."

I reached for it, my legs shaking a little. I was torn between the temptation to possess powerful magic and the fear of what would happen if I did.

They didn't know what I really was….

As soon as I clasped the crystal in my palm, I felt its dark, seductive power thrumming over me. "What does this do?" I asked.

"It charges your body with night magic. You must learn to channel it correctly, let it become one with your body. And once you do, you can leap from one place to another by communing with the darkness of shadows. Ruadan will help you learn to channel the magic effectively. He will need to see how you're able to handle the magic before you go further. Use the stone in the floor to anchor your feet, so the magic doesn't overwhelm you."

"What if…." I sucked in a sharp breath. How did I ask this question? How did I name this fear?

What if a dark, powerful magic infused me? What if there were worse things in the world than incubi?

What if I was one of them?

I cleared my throat, trying again. "What if this magic doesn't mix well with me? I don't know what my other half is." That old lie. Stick as close to the truth as possible. "What if I flip out and just start slaughtering everyone?"

"You won't." Bael nodded at Ruadan. "There is no better teacher."

I frowned, casting a doubtful glance at Ruadan. Like Bael, he had the rigid posture of a warrior. But without speaking, how was he supposed to teach me anything?

Whatever the case, I wasn't about to argue with the enormous, naked man in front of me. I'd just take his word for it.

Without another word, Bael turned and plunged into the portal.

Ruadan crossed over to the dark whirlpool, shadows intensifying around him. His cool, shadowy magic buzzed over my skin. The smell of burnt air rose in the room, like a thunderstorm after lightning strikes. I stared as the watery portal closed up again, replaced by a simple flagstone floor.

Once again, I'd failed to get a glimpse of the World Key, and my stomach sank.

Ruadan turned back to me, and he pulled the crystal from my hands. Then, he reached behind my neck, his powerful magic caressing my skin from my thighs up to my breasts and raising goosebumps over my arms. He clasped the necklace behind my nape.

As soon as he did, a rush of power flooded me, pooling in my chest and my belly like glacial waters. My back arched, and my mind went dark, until an image arose—

A field of fae corpses lay around me, skin blackening, turning gray....

I gasped at the wave of horror that washed over me.

Powerful hands clasped me by the waist, and the image dissipated. Ruadan had jumped, and he was standing behind me now, his powerful body pressed against mine. I slowed my breath, inhaling deeply. A thin sheen of sweat had bloomed on my skin, and my blood roared in my ears. But my mind was no longer flooded with disturbing memories.

Shadow magic curled from my fingertips. Somehow, with his touch, Ruadan was helping me channel that magic so that it didn't overwhelm my mind. It was as if his body helped to ground the magic in my mind. Now, with Ruadan's warm hands on my waist, his fingers over my hips, I could feel the shadow magic pulsing up my legs, skimming over my thighs.

But that disturbing image from the darkest depths of my memory still lingered, and another wave of shadow magic slammed into me.

CHAPTER 18

*M*y legs trembled. Even with Ruadan's help, I felt like my body was rejecting the shadow magic. I leaned back against his powerful form, my head tucked under his chin. Still, darkness clouded my mind once more. The next thing I knew, I was walking in those tall grasses, fae blood staining the soil....

Glaciers slid through my bones, wracking me with shivers. I was freezing from the inside out, teeth chattering.

Ruadan's arms slid tighter around me, encircling my waist. His embrace warmed me, and some of the shivering relented. He dispelled the disturbing memory from my mind.

Why was I thinking about those terrible memories now? I'd worked so hard to forget.

Heat radiated from Ruadan's powerful body into mine. When another surge of ice flooded my veins,

Ruadan's hands shot up, and he unclasped the crystal from my neck. He stepped in front of me, his brow furrowed.

Tremors wracked me, and I hugged myself. "I know. It's not working."

He pulled out a piece of paper and wrote on it.

We're going to start from the bottom up. Use the stone to anchor you.

I frowned. "What?"

He shoved the paper and pencil back into his pocket. Then, he put his hands on my hips and guided me back against a wall, pressing on my shoulders until they were flat against the stone. Warming me with his touch, he cupped my chin. He guided my head back against the wall until my spine lined up completely with the stone. I looked up at him, meeting his violet gaze, breathing in the smell of pine. So easy to get taken in by his stark beauty, so easy to forget what he really was—a cold-blooded killer.

"Why did you slaughter your last two novices?" I asked.

His fingers tensed on my hips, and for just a moment, shadows slid through his eyes until they darkened to pitch. And *there* was the shadow demon, eyes the color of the darkest hell. Icy dread raked a claw up my spine. That question *really* pissed him off for some reason.

"Quite handy, isn't it?" I said. "Only speaking when you want to."

He seemed to gain some mastery over himself, his

eyes shifting back to violet with silver flecks, and his muscles relaxed. I wasn't going to get an answer. Fine. I needed to remember that even if he was my mentor— and even if his magic felt delicious—I'd never be safe with him.

He grasped my hands in his, then turned my palms to face the wall. I understood the intent—I was supposed to keep as much of my body pressed firmly against the wall as possible, and use the contact with the stone wall to stabilize the magic. I splayed out my fingers over the stone.

Then, with his thumbs pressed into my hips, he straightened the small of my back against the wall. Ruadan's magic thrummed over my skin. Pressed against the wall, with my head tilted back, I felt strangely vulnerable before him.

Once again, he lifted the necklace. But this time, he clasped it around his own throat. It took me a moment to understand, but he was going to channel the power from his own body into mine, to act as sort of a conduit. That way, he could temper the intense torrent of magic. While I stood, pressed against the wall, he knelt before me.

For just a moment, I imagined that I was his queen, and he was my subject, and it gave me a little thrill. A smile curled my lips. But the feeling was quickly over when his fingertips met my ankles, sending an intense jolt of shadow magic into my blood.

When I peered down, I could actually *see* the tendrils of dark magic curling around my bare legs.

Slowly, Ruadan brushed his fingers over my ankles, then further up my calves. Every stroke of his fingers brought a rush of powerful tingles. Channeled through Ruadan, the power no longer overwhelmed me. It felt like an intense electrical rush over my skin.

Breathing in deeply, I tuned into the solidity of the rock behind my back, pressing myself firmly against the wall. It *did* work as a sort of anchor, diffusing some of the power of the shadow magic. Ruadan traced his hands further up my legs toward the hem of my dress, and my breath quickened at the feel of his hands on my thighs, under the hem. I trembled, the magic growing a little more powerful now. He spread out his fingers over my bare thighs. His touch felt distractingly *good* on my body, and my breath hitched.

As I looked into his eyes, I couldn't help the rush of molten heat that swept through my belly. His hands moved higher. My skin was warming, and I started to feel an overwhelming urge to crush myself against him. There were reasons this was a bad idea, but my thoughts had become too muddled for coherent thoughts. The air felt charged between us. My pulse raced, my mind no longer filling with dark memories. Now—much to my horror—my body was responding to him in a different way.

I stared at his mouth, wondering what it would feel like to kiss him. Something flared in his eyes, too. Was that desire snaking off his torso?

As his hands moved over me, his gaze roamed down my body. Slow, appreciative—as if he were imagining what I looked like without my dress on. His gaze lingered over my breasts, definitely taking notice of my hardening nipples beneath the fabric. My chest flushed with desire and embarrassment. He definitely *knew* how turned on I was right now, and there was no way to hide it.

Whatever he was thinking, it was no longer the cold, clinical look he'd given me before. His magic thrummed up my legs.

When I licked my lips, his gaze flashed to my mouth. His nostrils flared, fingers tightening on my hips. I thought of his canines at my throat, and bizarrely, the thought made me groan. Heat swooped through my core. My mind was blazing with a vision: Ruadan, spinning me around, grazing his canines over my neck. He'd rip off my knickers and fill me until I shuddered beneath him. Wild need overtook me, an ache building between my thighs.

Gods help me, some primal fae instinct was taking over and I *wanted* him desperately, even if the thought horrified me. I imagined my naked body sliding against his, his fingers stroking between my legs while I climaxed.

I knew he felt my desire when his eyes began darkening again, his own animal instincts taking over.

Night magic poured into me from his fingertips, and he pressed in closer. A stroke of his thumb on my hips—up and down, up and down—told me this was no longer just about magic, and the little moan I emitted confirmed it for him. He leaned in closer, his breath warming my neck. I was drawing him into my orbit, too.

His powerful shadow magic followed his hands up to my waist, and an intoxicating power pulsed in my core. Against my will, my back arched. I had to fight hard to remember to keep my fingers splayed against the wall, that I wasn't supposed to grip him by the hair and pull his mouth to mine.

Hands. Pressed. Against. The wall.

A vein in Ruadan's neck throbbed.

He ran one of his hands up my body, stroking up my back. Then he fisted my hair, his touch almost rough. With a dominating grip, he tilted my neck back, exposing my throat. My heart raced out of control. When he pressed his mouth to my neck, I moaned. His magic was distinctly, overwhelmingly sexual, and it had an intense effect on me.

He couldn't be an incubus, could he? Incubi loved pleasure. It's just that … he really felt like an incubus right now.

His other hand stroked me under the cotton fabric of my dress. It moved higher up over my ribs, magic pulsing from his hands—

Then, he froze.

He jerked his hands away from me as if I'd burned him. He pulled away, and his magic snapped out of my body.

It was at that moment that reality came crashing down on me. *My scars.* They were all over my ribs. The jig was up. No bar fight stories could explain that carnage.

I tried to catch my breath, staring at him.

How could I have let him get so close? Knowledge over someone was power, and now he knew more about me than I'd intended. It was his stupid, pretty face, plus some kind of animalistic fae instincts urging me to mate with him. I wasn't thinking clearly anymore, wasn't being tactical. I needed a much uglier mentor to get through this.

I loosed a long breath. I didn't think he'd directly connect me to Baleros. There'd been plenty of gladiator masters. Baleros just happened to be the cruelest.

Ruadan started writing on his paper, and I already knew what it would say before he handed it over.

Your body is covered in scars.

I crossed my arms, completely disoriented by the sudden absence of magic from my body, and also by the fact that, a few seconds ago, I'd been desperate to pull my clothes off.

I wasn't sure why tears stung my eyes, but it only made the situation more embarrassing. I didn't want him to know I'd been captured. I blinked, mastering control of myself, over my voice, before I answered. "Yep. From the arena."

I didn't want him to know me. Now, he was already looking at me differently, his eyes shining with something like pity. Exactly what I'd been dreading. Gladiators may have been fearsome warriors, but ultimately, we were slaves.

"You don't need to feel sorry for me," I snapped. "I

149

survived. I'm proud of my scars." Proud to have survived. Ashamed to have been captured in the first place.

He nodded, then I noticed his gaze sweeping up and down my body. I had the sense that he was reconsidering me in some way, but I wasn't quite sure how.

He nodded, then handed me another piece of paper.

I don't feel sorry for you. You're strong. Let's get back to training.

I loosed a slow breath. Good. That was over, and we could move on.

He gestured at the wall, and I understood I was supposed to back up against it again.

I pressed my legs, my spine, my fingers against the wall.

Ruadan began at my ankles once again. Working from the bottom up, his hands moved further up my legs—faster this time—and shadow magic surged along with his touch. A delicious, powerful magic tingled over my thighs, a hint of an electrical pulse that caressed me beneath my dress. His hands moved over my hips, my waist, leaving a rush of tingling magic in their wake. Night magic surged in my core. He brought his hands up further under my dress, his fingers just below my breasts.

Magic surged now, spilling from my ribs, out through my limbs, filling my fingertips, my toes, my head. Now, the magic felt like a part of me. Ruadan leaned in closer. He unclasped the necklace from his own neck.

His eyes locked on mine, pulsing with violet like the lumen crystal, and he secured it around my own neck.

Now, the power started to flood me again—darkness descending. But Ruadan wasn't leaving. His powerful body was pressed against me, eyes locked on mine.

His canines were bared, eyes darkening as a dark, primordial power filled us both. He leaned down, the side of his face brushing mine.

Night magic was an intoxicating rush. Before he knew what was happening, I found that my arms were around Ruadan's neck.

His hands slid around my thighs. I whispered his name. Now, his lips hovered just inches from mine. His sensual magic whispered through me, throbbing in my blood like a drug. He hoisted me up, his hands below my thighs, and I wrapped my legs around his waist. He pressed me against the wall, and a dark heat swooped through my belly. The desire definitely wasn't just coming from me. It crackled between us like an electric charge.

Night magic surged, and I felt at one with the dark, with the void, with the perfect silence of a midnight sky….

I stared into Ruadan's night-dark eyes, lost for a moment in the stark beauty of his features….

Baleros's seventeenth law of power: Never let an opportunity go to waste.

Then, a voice whispered in the back of my mind. Baleros's voice.

The World Key, the World Key, the World Key....

I had to see what was there. I reached for the collar of Ruadan's shirt, and I just started to tug it down....

Then, his body tensed, his eyes returning to violet. He lowered me again to the floor.

The piece of paper he handed me read,

Your body has been charged with night magic. We're done.

I was still catching my breath, aware of the embarrassing flush of my chest. "Is that how you train all your novices?" My voice came out a little sharp, and I wished I hadn't said anything at all.

He'd returned to his usual state—animal stillness, violet eyes that burned into me. He knew what I'd tried to do, that I'd been looking for the key.

I lifted the lumen crystal from my throat. "Fine. So what happens now? Are you going to teach me to shadow-run?"

A muscle twitched in his jaw. But instead of answering, he crossed out of the room.

I glared at the doorway after he left. He'd caught me trying to get a glimpse at the World Key, and now I was one step further away from earning his trust.

CHAPTER 19

*S*auntered across the Tower Green, sipping from my whiskey bottle on the way. A floral breeze kissed my skin.

I understood that the Shadow Fae reviled pleasure, but no one had taken away my whiskey yet, so for now, at least, it was my only real friend here.

As I walked, my heart was still racing out of control from the earlier encounter. At this point, I was nearly positive that Ruadan was an incubus, even if he didn't act like one. Incubi inspired lust, and they fed off it, too.

I gritted my teeth, angry with myself for letting him catch me looking for his World Key. Now, he wouldn't let me get anywhere near him. How angry was he, exactly? And what the fuck was I even looking for?

I needed some time to think. Since it seemed like he was attracted to me, maybe I could seduce him? Would he trust me that way? I wasn't sure. I wasn't exactly a romance expert, and I didn't know how to recreate the lust we'd felt in the tower room. I needed some more inspiration.

Instead of heading back to our shared room, I was making my way to the library. I pushed through a door, then climbed the dank tower stairwell until I reached the enormous hall.

My favorite Segway-riding librarian peered at me over the moon-shaped rims of her glasses, and I gave her a wave.

"Is there a romance section?" I asked.

She shook her head. "No. I have my own collection, of course, but those are private. We *do* have a romantic histories section."

"Fine. Can you show me where that is?"

She pointed to a wall in the library that was partially overgrown with moon flowers.

I crossed to it, clutching the straps of my backpack. Here, glittering moths dusted the books' spines. I sat on the ground before the stack, and I found an old favorite—a love story about a young knight, sent to fetch a wife for his rich uncle. But during their journey home, the two of them drank love potions. They fell in love with each other instead.

I chewed on my lip. What I needed was a love potion. If he were completely under the thrall of lust magic, I could get a glimpse under his shirt. Maybe I could even get him to tell me the truth in the heat of the moment.

I closed the book in my lap. I had no idea how to

make a love potion, and maybe I didn't need to rely on magic, anyway. The intensity I'd felt as we'd trained told me he wanted me without magic. Heat had crackled between us.

Seducing him was the best way to get to the World Key.

Despite the desire we'd both felt while training, I wasn't exactly a genius at seduction. I'd had a boyfriend before, but that had been the result of getting drunk in Rufus's bar, sleeping with a trumpet player, and then continuing to get drunk and sleep with the trumpet player until I realized we had absolutely nothing in common. Seduction was definitely not one of the skills taught at gladiator school. I'd literally spent my formative years in a cage. This was the sort of thing I'd have learned as a teenage girl if I hadn't been so busy stabbing people to death, and now I was completely behind the eight ball.

I rose and started crossing to the exit. What I really needed was a female friend….

Melusine didn't seem much like the seductive type, either, but she was a self-proclaimed genius.

I pushed through the door, heading out of the library into the glaring afternoon light.

As I crossed the Tower Green, I sniffed my way to Aengus's room, following Melusine's scent to a gleaming white tower.

Inside, I knocked on the door where her smell was the strongest. Melusine pulled it open. "Arianna. I wasn't expecting to see you here. I have been practicing three kinds of magic to prepare for our next trial."

"Oh, wow, that's very—"

"Shadow leaping, an explosion spell, and a second kind of explosion spell with more fire. What have you been practicing?"

I scratched my cheek. Talk about being behind the eight ball. "Not much yet. Is Aengus here?" I asked in a whisper.

"No." She opened the door further, motioning for me to enter.

Mahogany furniture ringed the room, and Aengus's bed looked as if it had been carved from a giant stag's antler. Here, a soft bed of moss grew on the floor, and a musky scent filled the room. I noticed right away that a second, smaller bed stood against one of the walls, and irritation simmered.

"You have a bed?" I snapped. "Ruadan didn't give me a bed."

She shrugged. "You sleep on the floor."

I folded my arms. "It would have been nice to have been offered one." I shook my head. "Sorry, I'm getting sidetracked."

"Are you here to ask about shadow-leaping?" She beamed. "You must have heard I'm very good at it."

"Um, not really. I was hoping you knew something about seduction."

She stared at me. "Do I seem like the type of person who would know anything about seduction?"

"Not particularly. Not at all, really. But you're the only woman here."

She cocked her head. "You *do* know that the knights are forbidden from taking on any lovers."

Conceal your true intentions.

I rolled my eyes. "Of course I know that. It's just that they're not forbidden from killing novices. And I thought—if I really need it someday—seducing Ruadan might be a reasonable protection against getting killed by him. You know, getting him to like me."

Her features cleared, and she eyed me dubiously. "I'm not sure if that makes sense."

"Obviously, it's not like we can have conversations," I pointed out. "Seduction is my only defense."

This seemed to convince her, and she nodded. "Yes. Of course. It's not the worst idea in the world." Her forehead creased as she thought about it. "You know, I don't think there's a lot to it. I don't think you have to do anything fancy. I think men just like naked women. And you're beautiful. I don't think it's more complicated than that."

"Really? So … I should get naked?"

"I believe so. Men like bared breasts, especially." She frowned at my chest. "And yours are fairly large."

"I mean, you're not wrong, and men definitely like breasts, but…." It couldn't be that simple, could it? And yet, the more I thought about it, the more I thought this sounded completely accurate. "Okay, thanks."

"Sure. I'll see you tomorrow night for the trial."

"Of course." Unless I managed to seduce the key away from Ruadan before then.

I FOUND Ruadan in his room, engaging in his favorite, super pro-social activity: knife-sharpening. His blade glinted, and he didn't even bother to look up at me as I crossed into the room.

Melusine's suggestion about bare breasts had seemed totally sensible in her room. But now, as I stood before a fae-demon who'd murdered his last two novices, I couldn't quite figure out how to just casually throw off my clothes without it being weird. Granted, Ruadan and Bael were fine with being naked, but it wasn't normal to me. I loved my body and I felt beautiful, but that didn't mean I'd just casually strip off in front of people.

I ran my fingertips over my ribs, where I felt one of the ridges of my scars. He'd offered to heal me before, hadn't he? Maybe that would be a sufficient pretense. The thing was, I didn't want them healed. I liked myself exactly the way I was, and each scar was a victory. But I'd do anything for Ciara.

Ciarianna would rise again.

I glanced in the gleaming reflection of one of his axes. I looked pretty enough, I thought. I pinched my cheeks a little to make them pink.

Ruadan was still looking down at his knives as he sharpened them. I took a deep breath. I sat at the edge of his bed and pulled off my boots. Then pulled off my dress, dropping it on a pile of my other clothes. The cold fortress air whispered over my skin as I stood in the middle of his room, just in my sheer black bra and knickers.

Ruadan was still looking down at his knives, pretending I wasn't in the room at all. I looked down at myself, then traced my fingertips over the ridge of a scar by my hipbone. A hellhound had caught me with an ax. I'd killed him by bashing his skull in with a rock. I was much more at home with that sort of mission than with the sheer bra sort of mission.

The boobs were sexy. The legacy of death maybe wasn't so much. But the scars were mine, and I hated to part with them.

Still, I crossed to Ruadan, and he lifted his gaze. His body went completely rigid at the sight of me. Sharp tendrils of his magic sliced through the air, menacing and ferocious.

Shadows darkened his eyes. I couldn't exactly tell if he liked what he saw or if he wanted to murder me in that moment, but either way, I felt completely vulnerable standing before him. The intensity of his gaze hit me like a wave of powerful magic, and my breath caught in my throat.

I touched one of the scars by my ribs. "You said you could heal me. Can you heal my scars?"

A long moment passed, and he eyed me with that eerie stillness. Then, he shifted and started writing on his piece of paper.

I will heal your new wounds. Not the old ones.

"Why?"

Because they don't need to be healed.

He was right. The wounds from the King of Mammon were still raw, and they hurt whenever I coughed or sat up too fast. The rest were just superficial. They didn't need to be healed.

"Fine."

He held out a hand to me, beckoning me closer, and I closed the distance between us.

As I stood in front of him, he brushed his fingertips over the wound on my abdomen. He curled one hand around me and it rested on my lower back. With the other, he traced over my skin around the cut. I stared as dark magic curled from his fingertips over my skin, snaking over the reddened marks. I was acutely aware of the fact that, with him sitting down and me standing up, my breasts were about level with his head. I couldn't quite pinpoint it, but something about the studied intensity with which Ruadan ignored my breasts suggested to me that he was actually completely focused on them. Melusine had been right.

The dull ache in my abdomen subsided completely.

The other new wound marred my hip, and I tugged down the side of my knickers to expose it. His hand on my back tensed, his other reaching for my hip. Before he touched my skin, his hand tightened into a fist, as if he were restraining himself. I was *definitely* having an effect on him.

I'm not sure what compelled me to do it, but I took another step forward, then slid into his lap.

Being this close to him, heat built within me. Now, his eyes were locked on mine as he traced his fingertips over my hip, inside my knickers. His magic stroked my body.

Then, as soon as he'd healed my second scar, he pulled his hand away from me, and he straightened.

I understood that was my cue to get off his lap. Fine. Boobs or not, seduction was not part of my skill set. But I was certain he'd felt something, and I was making some progress to getting closer to his chest.

I crossed back to my dress and pulled it on over my head. "So, are you going to teach me to shadow-jump?"

No key yet. But I could learn a new skill while I was at it. After I stole from the Seneschal, shadow-leaping might come in *very* handy.

CHAPTER 20

By Ruadan's side, I walked down a cobbled road in East London. To our left, an overground train line loomed over a dark park. Apparently, this is where I was supposed to practice shadow-leaping.

Ruadan wore not one, but two swords strapped to his back, doubling his intimidation factor. As we'd moved through the streets of East London, terrified humans had fled from our path.

We crossed into the grassy park, and a flicker of movement caught my eye. It took me a moment to register that I was staring at a man's naked arse, thrusting into the earth. When he looked back at us, terror paled his features, and he scrambled to stand and pull up his trousers.

"Uncle Darrell?" I whispered under my breath.

Ruadan must have heard me, because he turned to raise his eyebrows at me. I stared at Uncle Darrell, who was now sprinting across the park away from us. For a moment, I contemplated telling Ruadan that if he ever wanted to commune with the earth, he needed to bury the whole ballsack, not just the shaft. But I thought better of it as soon as I remembered that he had no sense of humor whatsoever.

Moonlight silvered the park, and mist curled around a few sparse trees. Under the elevated train track, shadows pooled in dark arches. Something about this place gave me the shivers, and I wanted to fill the silence.

"I've been here before," I said. "There's magic in this place."

We moved along a cobbled road that cut into the park. Dandelions dappled overgrown grasses. To our right stood brick walls that might be two centuries old. To our left, a rickety wooden house on stilts loomed over the train tracks—maybe a switching station at one time, long since abandoned. A small city farm stood on one side of the fields, complete with vegetable patches, chickens, goats, and a pig.

Acrid smoke rose from a burning car, probably stolen, abandoned in one of the Victorian train arches. "Not all magic comes from the gods or from spells," I said. "This is the magic of things that don't belong together. This is the magic of weird, forgotten places. Farms, burnt cars. Dandelions. Goats." I pointed to a tree, where sneakers dangled from the branches. Some crazy person had tied them there. "Shoes hanging like fruit from the boughs. See what I mean?"

Ruadan's eyes slid to me, and I thought I saw a sparkle of curiosity, but he was probably wondering if I'd lost my mind.

"I know," I said. "We have shadow-leaping to practice."

Ruadan pulled the glowing lumen stone from his pocket. Then, he stepped closer and clasped it around the back of my neck. His piney scent enveloped me.

As soon as the clasp shut, I felt that overwhelming rush of magical power. Darkness swam in my mind, but I managed to clamp down on my most disturbing thoughts.

Still, energy flooded me, and the coldness of the shadow void spilled through my veins and tendons like ink, freezing my bones. I stared up into Ruadan's cold, violet eyes. He didn't need a lumen stone at all, because this magic was part of him, as innate to him as walking was to me.

I tried channeling the magic, tried using the stones beneath me to ground it. And yet try as I might, it seemed as if a frozen void had opened up within my chest. An unending pit of ice. I'd mastered the power before, but now, my muscles started to seize up.

As soon as Ruadan put his hands on my waist, some of the panic began to subside.

I stared into his eyes, and I found the magic of night glimmering there.

Moonlight sculpted the perfect planes of his face. It unnerved me to have the full power of his gaze on me, but it excited me, too.

"Are you going to have to touch me every time I wear this lumen stone?" Sometimes I had a bad habit of nervously filling silence with chatter. "Because it might get weird when we're trying to fight the incubi and you have to keep sticking your hand up my dress."

No answer, of course. The coldness deepened within my chest.

Shut up, Arianna. Shut up.

I breathed in deeply, focusing on channeling the freezing magic throughout my body. Slowly, I started to absorb it and to disperse it more evenly.

Ruadan's eyes flared with silver. Once again, something was passing between us—an electrical charge, a pulsing, sexual energy. An intense ache burned through my body. He was *definitely* an incubus, and the heat of his sensual magic melted the coldness of the shadows within me.

He let out a low growl, fingers tightening on me. Then, with a move both quick and rough, he pulled me closer. He thrust his fingers into my hair and once more pulled my head back. His gaze pierced me.

This time, he crushed his lips against mine, and lust arced through me. His kiss was carnal, demanding. Heat shot through my belly as I responded to its unflinching ferocity. I opened my mouth, my tongue sliding against his.

The kiss deepened, growing wilder, and I ached for him. His grip on me tightened. Something about the intensity of the kiss made me feel like I was an answer to a question he'd been asking all his life.

His magic stroked my skin, licking between my legs, and hot ecstasy spiraled through me. I had no idea what was happening anymore, or how words worked, or what we were doing in the park. I just wanted more from him, wanted his tongue to swirl over my body.... Heat ignited in me, so powerful that it warmed the frigid pit in my chest. When he nipped my lower lip, my knees went weak, and I think I moaned.

But just as soon as it had begun, he pulled away from me. Of course, kissing was forbidden to a Shadow Fae. My breath was hitching in my throat, and I tried to slow my breathing even as my legs trembled.

He released his grip on me, and he took a step back, shadows snaking around him. Lust still flooded me. *Definitely* an incubus. I touched my lips, stunned that he'd kissed me at all.

My heart thundered against my ribs. *Play it off cool, Arianna. Play it off cool.*

"Not a big deal." I actually said those words out loud. "Just a kiss, whatever."

Like I said. When I was nervous, I tended to chatter.

If it was a tactic to help me control the magic, the kiss had worked. The coldness of the shadow magic no longer overwhelmed me. It surged along my skin, swirling through my muscles—an electric, crackling power. But I controlled it. The heat generated by Ruadan's lust magic had *definitely* countered the iciness of the shadow magic.

I looked down at my hands, at the soft wisps of dark magic that spiraled from my fingertips.

"You're an incubus, right?" I asked.

One nod confirmed my theory.

As an incubus, Ruadan controlled magic through sexual energy. That meant he could draw power from sexual energy, channel magic—heal from it, even. It also meant that he'd known exactly how turned on I'd been around him, which was slightly mortifying. Particularly since I had no idea whatsoever what he was thinking or feeling.

I folded my arms. "I thought incubi were supposed to enjoy themselves. You don't speak, don't drink alcohol, don't have lovers because the Institute won't allow it. You must be very conflicted."

A low growl told me it was time to drop the subject.

With a few deep breaths, I managed to master some of my overwhelming desire, but that kiss had knocked the ground out from under me. I'd been about twenty seconds away from stripping my clothes off right here in this park—even after I'd seen what Uncle Darrell had done to defile the poor earth.

I glanced at my fingertips, transfixed by the smoky magic that curled from them.

To my surprise, Ruadan reached out and lifted my chin so that I was meeting his startling gaze. Then, he pointed to the farm—at a goat pen, in fact.

"Okay. You want me to jump into the goat pen?" Magic sizzled over my skin. Maybe Bael had been right, and Ruadan was an excellent mentor in his own weird, slightly insane way. After all, I now possessed powerful magic, and I was about to learn how to use it.

And yet…. "Before I jump into the goat pen, can we talk about the thing where you murdered two of your novices? Is that right, or was it just a rumor?"

When he started writing on the piece of paper again, I fully expected it to come back with some kind of denial.

Instead, what he handed back to me was simply the word:

Executed.

No other explanation. No excuses or context. Just a stark reminder of what was at stake here. If I failed to impress the Shadow Fae, I'd be executed. If I stole from them and ran off with the key, I'd be executed.

And yet if I didn't, Ciara would die.

While I was mulling over this shitty predicament, Ruadan touched my arm. He pointed once more at the farm, urging me to jump.

"Right. To the goat pen." I stared across the field, at the goats, unable to conceive how I could just shift myself over there. Bael had said that I would be jumping from one shadow to another by connecting to the shadow's darkness. Since it was nighttime, shadows surrounded us, but I wasn't exactly sure how to meld with them.

All I knew was that the first step would be to move away from Ruadan, whose masculine scent was distracting me.

I took a few steps away from him, breathing in the night air. I picked through the scents of burning rubber and leather from the car, the chicken coop, the grass, the pigpen, the goat fur, the old chicken bones someone had left out nearby ... the dozens of other smells. I tuned in just to that burnt air smell. That was the smell of shadow magic.

I stared at the uneven wood of the goat pen, my gaze locked in on the pool of darkness in one corner.

Magic crackled over me, and coldness spilled through my blood. I let my mind go blank, filling with shadows. Mentally, I felt myself meld with the darkest corner of the pen. Then, I leapt.

I slammed into a wooden gate post and fell back on my arse in the mud.

The goat brayed. With a jolt, I realized the fucker was running for me, his bell ringing. As I jumped to my feet, he head-butted me, and I fell back again. A goat hoof trampled on my hand. For a fraction of a second, I considered punching him, but there was definitely something morally dubious about punching a goat in the face.

As I struggled to stand with the goat smashing into me, knocking me off balance, my gaze flicked back to the park. I let my mind fill with shadows, my sights locked on the dark point beneath an apple tree. I communed with that shadow, and the darkness within me connected to it. In the next moment, I was there, free from my goaty attacker.

Then, I focused on Ruadan. In the night, he appeared like a pool of ink, two vibrant violet eyes peering out from a void. Like a black hole, the Wraith sucked in light and trapped it within his sphere.

I tuned into his shadows, to the dizzying, icy power within them, and I jumped. I slammed into Ruadan, and it was like hitting a brick wall. I stumbled back, but this time, I managed to regain my balance.

I crossed my arms, glaring at him. "Did you know that goat would attack?"

Seriously. *No* idea why I kept asking him questions at this point.

Ruadan reached behind his back, drawing his two longswords. He handed one to me.

I grasped it by the hilt. I was *much* more comfortable with the sword than I was leaping around goats. But I was pretty sure I knew what Ruadan wanted me to do.

"You want me to fight you while we're shadow-leaping, right?" I asked.

Ruadan nodded.

I had to admit, the idea of mastering this skill was thrilling. This would be an astounding advantage in a fight against someone who couldn't use it. Only problem was, it depended on me having access to a lumen stone. Baleros didn't have one, and I was guessing they weren't easy to come by.

But since I was planning on stealing from Ruadan anyway, what was one more, little item?

CHAPTER 21

I didn't get too much time to contemplate my future heist, because a cold current of air whooshed beside me, and Ruadan was gone.

I scanned the darkness until my gaze landed on the cold glint of steel—Ruadan's sword, across the park. I tuned into his shadows, then leapt to him. Once again, I overshot the mark, slamming into his chest. I stumbled back again, and his hand gripped my waist for just a moment before he released me.

It was starting to become clear that I needed to focus on the shadows around Ruadan, or I'd keep overshooting and ramming into the stone wall of his chest.

Then, another cold whoosh of air, his sword glinting twenty feet away. This time, I jumped to the shadows two feet behind him and swung my sword. But once again, he'd anticipated my moves. He parried, blocking my strike, then jumped away.

Always anticipate your enemy's actions.

Ruadan continued to jump away, each time anticipating where I'd land just moments later. We shifted around, moving from the dark archways to the train tracks over the park. I nearly tumbled off the house on stilts before I regained my balance. We jumped again to an abandoned train station, then to the shoe tree.

Just like before, Ruadan kept demonstrating an uncanny ability to predict what I was about to do next. Almost as if we had been trained by the same person.

Had Baleros been Ruadan's mentor at one time?

I needed to surprise him. I'd improved my skill already. I was no longer slamming into his chest. Since we were using longswords, we needed to be a few feet apart to parry, and each time, I landed just the right distance from him, quickly assuming my fighting stance. But maybe I didn't have to use my weapon like a sword.

Ruadan leapt away, and I glimpsed his vibrant eyes in the darkness. I melded with the shadows just behind him. With a blur of speed, I brought my sword to his throat. It required standing on my tiptoes, pressed against him, which wasn't the most stable position.

I whispered, "Drop the sword, pretty boy."

Instead, he gripped my hand, pulling it down. Then, he ducked down to slip under my arm—a smooth, lightning-fast gesture.

Instantly, he was behind me, pinning my arms. I struggled against his grip for a moment. Then, I realized he was trying to communicate something to me.

He slid his hand down to my sword hand and

pulled my weapon from me. Then, he handed me a dagger. A misericorde, to be precise. I wasn't quite as skilled with daggers as I was with a sword, which might have been why we'd started in familiar territory. But I'd used stiletto knives plenty, and this wasn't wildly different. Usually, misericordes were used for a final death stroke to a wounded gladiator—not for combat—but you could kill with it. Its name meant something like *act of mercy,* an end to suffering.

I stepped away from Ruadan's grasp and turned the dagger around in my hand. "Is this what we'll be using?" I asked.

He nodded.

"It's not the best weapon to fight with…." I frowned, thinking it over. If we were fighting incubi, we wouldn't be killing them. Incubi were immortal.

Slowly, understanding began to dawn. Hellhounds and other reaping demons had special tools they used to reap souls for their gods—to send them to one of the seven hells. Enchanted pens, daggers, and other sharp objects created by the gods themselves.

We wouldn't be using daggers to assassinate, but to reap their souls. Once we stabbed an incubus, he'd be sent straight to the shadow hell—the void.

"A reaping dagger, right?"

Ruadan nodded.

"Please tell me we're practicing with fake ones."

He nodded again.

Good. That meant if we accidentally stabbed each

other while we were practicing, we wouldn't end up in the shadow hell.

Before I could ask another question, Ruadan was off again, shadow-leaping to the abandoned tracks.

We jumped and whooshed all over the park, blocking each other's attacks. We whirled through the darkness, slowly getting to know each other's quirks. Ruadan had a certain rhythm to his movements, moving slowly then fast again, and I started to be able to anticipate his jumps. He was aggressive but controlled, striking diagonally, aiming for my shoulder each time. Occasionally, he'd arc around to the side. Either he was certain I'd parry each strike, or he felt *very* confident in his healing skills, because he didn't seem to be holding back.

Our pace sped up, and I moved like a lunar wind, skimming over the ground. The faster I moved, the more the magic started frosting my veins, and emptiness welled between my ribs. Apparently, there was a limit to how much shadow magic I could channel at one time, and my legs began trembling.

Baleros's thirteenth law of power. Don't let your opponent see your weaknesses. And never admit defeat.

The shadow magic sent my teeth chattering, but I didn't want to relent, not while Ruadan was still leaping from shadow to shadow, evading me. I needed to keep going, to prove to him I wasn't just a bar-brawling, whiskey-swilling waste of space.

Crush your enemy completely.

I let the shadow magic flood me, surging through

my bones. As I flew across the park, emptiness billowed in my chest, and my mind flashed with images of a dirt floor, the bottom of a cage. Twelve dead fae by my feet, skin rotting, turning black….

The void was eating at me, and long-buried memories started to surface. Once, Baleros had given me a butterscotch sweet. I had been seventeen, far too old to be impressed by sweets, but I'd snatched it up from the dirt. I'd kept it with me in the cage, refusing to eat it.

You have a pathetic tendency to grow attached to anyone who shows you the smallest bit of kindness.

Baleros was right about me.

Cold fury erupted. I gritted my teeth, fighting to control the shadow power. I wanted blood. I wanted to win.

I had a vague sense that Ruadan wanted to stop, now, that the training was over, that I'd lost control of the magic, but Baleros's voice rang in my head.

Crush your enemy completely.

Our swords sparked like stars in the night sky until a blast of frosted air whipped around me. My skin felt like cracking ice.

I wanted to leap again, but I'd lost track of Ruadan. Then, two powerful arms clamped around my torso, pinning my own arms down, and Ruadan's muscled body pressed hard against me from behind.

His grip dominated me, and he squeezed my wrist hard until I dropped my dagger. It clanged against the stones.

At this point, I realized how violently I was shaking.

From behind me, Ruadan reached under my shirt and pressed his palm flat against my belly. Slowly, the flood of shadow magic began to even out again, and I slumped against him. Still, the surge of magic had depleted all of my energy, and my eyes were already starting to close.

Ruadan slipped an arm under my back, one under my legs as he lifted me.

And then, I rested my head on his powerful chest, and breathed in the scent of pine.

I WOKE on Ruadan's cold flagstone floor. Nectarine light poured in through the windows. Was it sunrise? No, the sun didn't hit this side of the building in the morning. I blinked. Sunset, then. I'd slept a very long time.

I reached for the pendant at my throat, only to realize someone had taken it off before laying me down.

I rubbed my eyes, and it took me a few seconds to realize that a blanket covered me. And a *pillow*—a gods-damned pillow lay on the floor.

I glanced across the room to find Ruadan dressing, strapping a series of knives to his waist.

Had he really given me a blanket and pillow? It was the first really kind thing he'd done for me. It was the first indication that he cared about my comfort beyond just seeing me survive as part of his duty. I lifted the blanket to my nose, breathing in the scent of pine.

I scanned the room. A pie stood on the table, steam curling from its crust, and my stomach rumbled. Had he got me food as well? Last night, when we'd trained in the park, a sort of battle fury had taken over me. Ruadan had been my enemy. But what if he wasn't? What if he actually liked me?

But as soon as I glanced at the arsenal on his wall once more, I froze. I was doing it again. My tendency to grow pathetically attached to anyone who showed me the smallest bit of kindness. Something sharp and cold pierced my chest.

Last night in the park, I'd felt completely over-whelmed by our kiss. It had ripped the world out from under my feet and left me in a free fall. But of course, it had just been part of the training, a way to get me to channel shadow magic. If Baleros had been able to channel magic that way, he would have. Now, I was letting Ruadan toy with my emotions.

Ruadan was being kind. And what had Baleros taught me about kindness? It gave a mentor power over their student. It made the recipient a slave.

Think about this carefully, Arianna. What had he done with his last two novices? He'd executed them. His own words. He'd execute me if he thought it necessary. As soon as Grand Master Savus gave the order, Ruadan would have my neck on the block, iron sword raised. He'd take my head clean off. He'd told me this much.

So what were the blanket and the pillow for?

He was Balerosing me, again. He fought like Baleros. He used my old master's moves. He'd trained with Baleros—maybe was even trained by Baleros. And this was my fucking butterscotch sweet, the pathetic trinket I'd cling onto at the bottom of a dirt cage. This was my strawberry. The smallest bit of kindness….

I rose, my legs shaking, picking up the blanket as I did.

"I don't need a fucking blanket," I shouted. "Or a pillow. Got it?"

Ruadan whirled.

"I sleep on the floor. I look after myself. That's how it's always been, and that's how it always will be. I don't need this fucking pillow." Anger flooded me, and I threw it at him. I knew how this worked. He'd throw me a few tokens, and I'd be his to control until it was time to lay my head on the chopping block. The betrayal would kill me before the blade ever did. I wouldn't let that happen. I wouldn't let myself die inside. "I don't need your fucking butterscotch sweets."

Ruadan's brow furrowed, surprise etched across his perfect features.

Point one to me, Baleros. Never let your enemy anticipate your actions. Ruadan had definitely not been expecting me to yell at him about butterscotch sweets.

"It's a metaphor," I explained. *Careful, Arianna. Careful.* I couldn't let him know how well I knew Baleros. Already, my rage was fizzling out. "Never mind. I just don't need a blanket. I can sleep on the floor, and please don't pretend to be nice to me because I know what you're doing."

Now, he looked irritated, and he pointed sharply at the pie, shadows whipping around him in savage arcs. Apparently, he'd heard my stomach rumble, and he'd assessed—correctly—that at least part of my fury had to do with my hunger.

I crossed to the table. "Thanks for the food. I understand that you need to keep me fed and to keep me from freezing to death."

I sat down at the stone table, my mouth already watering. Potato and leek pie with gravy this time. Gods below, I no longer cared if he was trying to manipulate me, I wanted to wrap him up in my arms for getting me this pie. It melted in my mouth, rich and buttery.

"So I slept all day," I said.

He nodded, then sat across from me, his enormous form looming over the table.

My limbs still ached. "I guess the shadow magic burned me out a little."

It was actually damned lucky I'd been paired with Ruadan. While all of the other novices had been training with magic since birth, I'd needed a part incubus to help me manage the full force of the magic. Someone to unfreeze me a little.

Ruadan pulled out a piece of paper, and he wrote:

While you're focused on crushing your opponent, you're letting the magic overwhelm you. Remember to ground the magic in the earth below you, so you don't burn out.

"I'll be fine." I took another bite of the pie. "So, when do we go after this nest of incubi?"

In a few hours.

I leaned back in my chair. I wasn't exactly ready for this, but I'd gone into battle unprepared before. And I'd lived.

I glanced at the pillow on the floor, and the feathers that had tumbled onto the stone. Somehow, the damn pillow—that little hint of kindness—scared me more than the incubi.

CHAPTER 22

*U*nder one of the dark arches—in the same park where I'd practiced with Ruadan—I stood in a line of novices. We were waiting for Grand Master Savus's arrival to give us the reaping command. The burnt car from last night had stopped smoking and now stood, blackened, among the other rubbish in the archway—old fridges, a children's plastic shopping trolley. Newspapers, egg cartons, and abandoned sneakers lay strewn around our feet.

And Aengus had promised me a life of glamour among the Shadow Fae.

From what I understood, the incubus nest wasn't far from here. In fact, somewhere nearby, they'd taken over a nightclub.

Maddan narrowed his eyes at my skimpy clothing—a short skirt, a low-cut silk shirt, and no bra. "Whore," he whispered.

Fuckwit. I wasn't going to argue with him, because it

served no purpose. He had no idea what he was in for, anyway.

The fae males had no gods-damned clue that they were at a distinct disadvantage for this trial. None of the males had any idea how nightclubs worked in the human realm. They'd never been to a bar, or stood outside trying to get into an exclusive nightclub by showing just the right amount of cleavage. They probably planned to simply waltz up to the door and demand entry. They'd concealed their pointed ears and left the oak leaves at home. But beyond that, they wouldn't fit in at all.

Melusine and I, on the other hand, were perfectly attired for the occasion. Our skimpy clothing was our ticket into the incubi's nightclub.

I brushed my fingertips over the misericorde reaping dagger concealed by my side.

If the fae males somehow managed to get into the club, the advantage would shift. Incubus lust magic only worked on females. Melusine and I could possibly end up wildly distracted.

In any case, the most important thing to remember for tonight's trial was that one stray prick of our daggers would mean an eternity in hell. If we accidentally stabbed ourselves, it was straight to the void forever. And that might explain why the males were a little bit jumpy this evening.

The barguest growled. "Once you get in the club, whores, and sniff that incubus magic, you'll be rutting like bitches in heat."

"Are you suggesting that I'm dog-like? You literally transform into a—" I sighed. "Never mind." Not even worth it. He was an idiot, and he probably wouldn't survive this task.

The barguest growled again, but the echoing of footfalls in the archway and the thickening of mist cut him short.

Grand Master Savus stepped out of the archway's shadows, and the novices went quiet. A steady stream of water droplets dripped from above.

I shoved my hand into my pocket, brushing my fingertips over the lumen crystal. Someday, when I was living as a fugitive, the crystal would be mine.

Savus prowled before us. "Tonight, you will be reaping souls in a crowded nightclub. We will be watching to see how you perform. Stealth, efficiency, and discretion will be noted. Commoners fear us, but we do not like to call attention to ourselves more than necessary. If humans become too afraid, they will grow restless. Agitated. Our fragile alliance will crumble. Humans can be so irrational. What's more, you are novices. You are not Knights of the Shadow Fae. You may not present yourselves as Knights of the Shadow Fae. Tonight, you will disguise yourselves as humans."

Savus steepled his fingers.

"You all have your lumen stones, yes? Please be aware that these are extremely valuable. Any novice who loses their lumen stone can expect to meet their end with the blade of an iron ax."

Crikey. I was starting to think the knights were a little overeager to get the iron axes out.

I clasped the necklace around the back of my neck, and my body surged with an icy jolt of shadow magic. Just as Ruadan had instructed, I used the stones beneath my feet to ground the power, channeling the magic evenly. I sucked in a deep, shaking breath as the power imbued my muscles and bones.

Savus crossed to the archway's opening, pointing to the street that lined the far end of the park. "Find the incubi's nightclub. Enter discreetly, posing as humans. Reap incubus souls. Remember—we kill in the shadows. And if you don't remain discreet, you will likely end up dead. We believe many incubi lurk in there, and they will slither from the shadows to slaughter you if they discover your presence. Don't cause a scene."

I shot a glance to the barguest, once again convinced he'd die before the night was over. I could not say the thought brought me distress.

"Wait until I issue the command," Savus cautioned.

Along with the shadow magic in my veins, adrenaline arced through my blood. When I glanced at the other novices, starlight seemed to spark in their eyes. The magic of Nyxobas pulsed through us, just as it did with Ruadan.

The barguest growled low under his breath. Shadows whipped violently around Maddan—the prince—tinging his auburn hair with darkness. A cold night wind rippled over my body, and I drew my dagger from its sheath.

By my side, Melusine was muttering to herself. *Enter silently, send them all to hell. Enter silently, send them all to hell. Enter silently, send them all to hell.*

Her mumblings, combined with her sweet face, had a deeply unnerving affect.

I turned to Melusine, whispering audibly, "Maddan is probably going to do something stupid, like miss the goat pen altogether."

Melusine frowned, ready to argue with me that we *should* miss the goat pen, that the goat was a belligerent monster who'd slam us into the mud repeatedly, worse than the incubi. But I held up a finger to silence her. Understanding dawned on her features, and she laughed a little too loudly. "Haha. Yeah. He'd be just that stupid. Miss the goat pen."

I stared across the park, beyond the farm, where the streetlights twinkled. With the coldness of the shadow magic chilling me, I wanted their warmth. I longed for light right now.

"Now," said Savus. "Go forth and reap."

Shadows spilled through my blood like ink, and I mentally fused with the pool of darkness just before the goat pen. I jumped, zooming through the air and landing softly in the wet grass outside the fence.

The barguest hurled himself into the pen, landing just before the goat, who immediately slammed into him. Of course he was the stupidest one.

Melusine and I were already moving on, jumping beyond the farm, toward the yellow streetlights.

Savus hadn't told us where to find the nightclub,

and that was part of the test. As we moved closer to the main street, I sniffed the air, tuning into the smell of electric magic. It was the lightning-storm smell of night magic and of incubi. As I jumped into a shadowy alleyway on the main street, I homed in on the shadow magic—powerful under the smell of beer, sweat, and rubbish.

Graffitti-covered walls lined either side of a narrow main street. With its streetlights and club signs, there were fewer shadows, but I found them behind a line of food trucks, and by zigzagging across the street into narrow alleyways.

Partygoers staggered down the road, some of them singing loudly. I knew this neighborhood—it was one where everyone went to get completely hammered, and I was quickly realizing that we didn't need to worry about discretion too much. You could run down this street in a flaming squirrel costume and most people wouldn't notice.

As I moved, I smelled the mossy scent of fae, and I caught a glimpse of bright red swooping past me.

Dammit. Maddan was getting ahead of me. Oh well. Let him burn himself out. He wasn't getting into the club, and maybe I could just let him lead me to it.

I tracked his movements to a dark alleyway that cut between two Victorian brick buildings. The prince was right on target, because the scent of incubi grew stronger here. In fact, I could already feel their magic sweeping over my skin in a rush of tingles. Even outside the club, my body was heating. No wonder they'd attracted a long line of human females. It was starting to become clear to me that infiltrating a nest of incubi would be distracting as hell, but at least Ruadan wasn't lingering around, making it worse with his stupidly beautiful face.

In the alleyway, the humans chatted to each other and toyed with their cell phones. Despite the fact—or perhaps because of the fact—that no sign marked the entrance to the incubi's club, this was apparently the hottest spot in the city tonight.

Maddan strutted on in front of me, every inch the royal fae. He'd left his oak leaves home tonight, but with his rigid posture and imperious glare, he still looked like a weirdo among the humans.

Getting into the club wasn't as easy as just shadow-leaping inside. You had to see a spot in order to shadow-jump to it, and a brick wall blocked our entrance—not to mention the two bouncers built like brick shit-houses. We were disguised as humans, but even if we weren't, the bouncers might not care. In London, nightclub bouncers might be the single group of humans unafraid of spell-slayers.

I glanced behind me, relieved to find that Melusine had followed hot on my heels, spine straight to emphasize her boobs. The girl was smart, even if she literally couldn't use a sword to save her life.

The barguest and Sea Monster shoved past us. Already, I could see the bouncers scowling at them. No way in hell were these fae males getting inside the front entrance. Unless they wanted to slaughter some humans in front of a crowd, they'd be forced to skulk below-ground, trying to find a way in through the sewers.

I hung back a little, so the bouncers didn't think Melusine and I were with those three twats. From here, I couldn't quite hear what Maddan was saying, but I'm *sure* it was something totally normal and human sounding, like, "Maddan, Carver of Enemies, son of Wanktonius of the House of Knob-Endians."

Whatever he said, one of the bouncers was already shoving him in the chest. I could practically *see* the steam coming off Maddan. Right now, he was probably considering reaping this bouncer's soul and just rampaging into the club. Certainly, the barguest's hand was looking twitchy by his sheathed dagger. If only Savus hadn't cautioned us to work in the shadows….

"In the shadows," I whispered loudly.

The barguest turned, snarling. Already, they were fucking up the discretion thing, and I hoped Savus was seeing this.

I took a step closer, until I could hear what Maddan was saying, and just caught the end of, "probably full of whores anyway," before the bouncer landed a hard punch on his cheek.

All three fae males snarled, before finally mastering themselves. I grinned at them as they skulked past us, dismissed by the bouncers. That was one big "enter silently" fail.

I leaned over to Melusine, whispering, "Time to unleash the holy trinity of nightclub bouncer approval:

blogging, boobs, and banging the DJ. Or, in my case, pretending to have banged the DJ."

She cocked her head, frowning, and blinked her large, brown eyes. She had no idea what I was talking about.

Not a big deal. She'd given me a strawberry, and now she was my plus-one.

I sauntered over to the bouncers, swaying my hips and twirling a strand of my lavender hair around my finger.

"Hey, guys." For reasons I couldn't quite explain, I adopted an American accent for this. Maybe Americans were just sexier somehow. "I'm writing a piece for the Hot Nights in London blog. I spoke to someone earlier about coming in to do a piece on your herbal gin and tonics."

I didn't have to research that one. Every bar in London—even the shitty one where I'd worked—was doing herbal gin and tonics. In our case, we basically mixed some cheap oregano with Tesco Dry Gin, but an incubus club probably used hothouse cucumbers, freshly farmed rosemary, and a dusting of gold on the rim.

One of the bouncers scowled at me. "You spoke to someone, you said? Who was it?"

"My friend Gary, the DJ. We're very, very close friends." I actually *did* know of a DJ named Gary. I'd never met him, but he played every club in East London. He was something of a legend. "I know Gary" had basically become a password for entrance to any of Shoreditch's clubs.

"Everyone says they know Gary," countered the bouncer.

Shit. It was becoming harder these days.

"Yeah, but I *actually* know him. He's tall, slouches a lot, wears baggy T-shirts, often smells like spliffs, rambles about government conspiracies, and carries around a bag of records," I said, describing literally every DJ who had ever existed.

The bouncer nodded, squinting at me as he considered my proposition. "He's actually very proud of his fitted black T-shirts."

Okay. *Almost* every DJ.

"If you know him so well," the bouncer went on, "what's he calling himself these days?"

It just so happened that I knew the answer to this, since I'd prepared weeks ago to get into an exclusive club for a "clothes swapping and suds night." Don't ask.

"He goes by Gary the Tall, sometimes," I said. "Also known as Gazza."

The bouncer shook his head, unimpressed.

"All right." He unhooked the velvet rope, stepping aside.

And point one goes to the ladies.

Melusine smiled at me, and we crossed into a long hallway lit by glowing blue stones embedded into the walls. At the end of the hallway, a silver door blocked our way, carved with the sigil of the Night God: a circle with a dot in the middle—basically a giant tit—next to a crescent moon. These demons weren't even trying to hide their demonity. They were just throwing it in the knights' faces. I almost felt a sense of umbrage before I remembered I had no intention of actually becoming a knight.

Before I could grab the door handle, Melusine grabbed my arm. "Enter silently, send them to hell."

CHAPTER 23

*B*efore I pushed through the engraved door, I peered at Melusine. "Are you ready for this?"

"Yes." She sucked in a deep breath. "It's just that I prepared my whole life for this. I've been practicing magic and Angelic spells since I was a little girl. Believe it or not, I don't have many friends. I used to draw faces and tape them to broom handles so I'd have someone at my birthday parties. I'm not good with people. I'm not even good with the broom people. At least three of them hated me, and I could never get them to eat the cake…. If I fail here, I have nothing to go home to." Her brow creased. "And if you fail, they'll execute you. We both have a lot to lose. But only one of us can get a spot. None of this is good news."

A deep, throbbing bass pulsed through the door.

My jaw tightened. This wasn't the best time for this discussion. "Look, Melusine. We just need to take this

192

one step at a time. Today, we just need to survive and reap some souls. We'll figure out the rest tomorrow. We're both survivors. You survived extreme loneliness." And I survived the gladiator ring. "We'll both make it through this."

She nodded, and I pulled open the door into a scene of pure hedonism. The club wasn't what I expected. I'd been expecting flashing lights, a large dance floor. Instead, it looked like an enormous, Victorian opium den. Persian rugs covering the floors, dark wooden alcoves with pillows and chaise lounges, silky drapes, candle-lit chandeliers…. Fire hazards all over the place, but none of the people making out in the alcoves seemed to care.

A curving wooden stairwell swooped up to a mezzanine floor overhead. In the balconies above us, I caught glimpses of naked women straddling men, some lying beneath them. People were dancing lasciviously to the strange, pulsating music, crackling from an old phonograph. Gary stood behind it in his fitted black T-shirt, rifling through a crate of albums.

So far, I saw humans everywhere, but I could feel the magic of the incubi all around us. Incubi's magic was twofold—they both fed off female sexual energy and could stimulate it. If the males ever made it in here, they'd have a huge advantage over us.

Still, it wouldn't be too hard to go unnoticed, because *no one* would be paying attention to us. They had far more interesting things to focus on.

I breathed in deeply, homing in on the scent of

incubi. They were near, but not on this floor. I scanned the mezzanine, catching a glimpse of dark, leathery wings. *There.* With Melusine by my side, I crossed deeper into the club, trying to act casual while mentally tallying the incubi on the floor above.

My skin was growing hot, and I stared at a couple who lay on top of a table. The woman—a brunette with long legs—was straddling a powerfully built human man. His hands were sliding over her arse, and for just a moment, I gaped at them.

A smack to my arm pulled me out of my reverie. "Move silently, send them all to hell. *Now.*"

"Right."

I didn't have time to talk strategy with Melusine before she jumped away from me. For a few moments, I tracked her movements, impressed with her speed. So *that's* why they'd recruited her. She was brilliant with a lumen crystal.

Then, it was time to do some reaping of my own. I stalked into the shadows of an empty alcove, and I pulled my reaping dagger.

From there, I jumped into the shadows in the stairwell, whooshing up the stairs until I reached the mezzanine floor. From the upper level, I scanned the balconies. Silently, in the shadows, Melusine had already taken out two of the incubi. *Nicely done, girl.*

By the time the male novices got in here, there'd be nothing left for them. But I didn't have too much time to gloat about that thought, because I had souls to reap.

My gaze landed on an incubus in one of the balcony

alcoves. He lay back on a chaise lounge, his leather wings swooping behind him. A red-haired woman lay on top of him, her body glowing and writhing. How was Melusine keeping the consorts silent?

She wasn't much of a killer, so she must've been using magic to knock them out. I didn't have those skills, but I did know how to choke a human out—just enough that she'd lose consciousness, but not enough that she'd die. My skillset was a little rougher than Melusine's.

Cold, electric magic whispered up my spine, and I jumped to a shadow in the alcove. The magic of lust was overpowering, heating up my core, and I struggled to focus. I took one step closer to the couple….

A wave of lust slammed into me. My pulse began racing, and I took a step back into the shadows, trying to master myself with slow breathing. I willed my heart rate to slow. Melusine was doing a lot better with this, but that girl was so tightly wound I wasn't sure she ever felt desire.

Either that, or she was thinking of her sad broom-people birthday parties. In fact, just the image of Melusine crying while trying to force a broom person to eat birthday cake was enough to drive the lustful thoughts right out of my mind.

I took another step forward and threw the dagger, landing it in the incubus's heart. Immediately after throwing it, I clamped my hand over the woman's mouth and pinched her nose shut.

She struggled against me, trying to scream. I let go

as soon as she stopped struggling, and she slumped to the floor, unconscious. Her chest still rose and fell. Messier than whatever Melusine was doing, but it got the job done.

When I scanned the balcony again, I spotted another incubus—one I hadn't seen before. He was dancing, dressed in a long, velvet bathrobe. He had a thin, curly mustache and a glass of champagne in his hand. A naked woman sidled up to him, wrapping her arms around his neck.

Gods *damn,* these women were not making my job easy. They were just trying to have a good time, and I couldn't justify killing them. I had *some* kind of moral code, after all.

I waited until she pulled away from him, dancing on her own. She lifted her arms over her head and swayed her hips, eyes closed in ecstasy. Then, I summoned the shadow magic, that cold rush of power.

I jumped, landing just behind the woman. One hand over her mouth and nose, the other to throw the dagger. It landed in the incubus's throat, and he collapsed. *Say hello to Nyxobas for me.*

The woman was trying to elbow me in the stomach, and she got a few jabs in, but I held on tight until she stopped bucking, and she slid to the floor.

I breathed in deeply. We'd reaped a few incubi souls, but by the heat surging in my blood, I knew there were plenty more. We just had to find them. Only—we didn't have a ton of time before the women I'd smothered woke up, or someone stopped fucking long enough to notice all the bodies lying around the place.

I crossed out of the alcove into a dimly lit corridor of dark wood with doors inset into the walls. Candles flickered in sconces, casting dancing shadows over silky sheets and pillows strewn across the floor.

The farther I walked down the corridor, the more desire built in my body, and even my skimpy clothing felt too tight, too restrictive. That meant I was moving closer to the incubi.

Sensuality throbbed in my core, and my hips started to sway as I walked, nipples brushing against the silk of my top. I had an overwhelming urge to pull it off. I had to stop my hand from inching down between my thighs….

Arianna. Focus on finding the incubi in front of you.

Except, why did I feel like the waves of desire were coming from behind me, now?

I whirled, my dagger ready. But it wasn't incubi that I found.

No, it was the three fae douchebags, slinking around the dark corridors, their clothing sodden from the underground sewer system. Maddan stepped forward, violet light glowing between his fingertips. What the hell was that?

"You didn't leave any incubi for us to reap, did you? This is why females should not be allowed in the Institute. You've used your feminine wiles to your advantage."

I blinked. "Oh, I must have missed the part about

how you needed special treatment because of your overwhelming incompetence, but it does make sense now that you mention it."

Maddan just cocked his head. "Where did you learn to fight as well as you do, gutter fae? You didn't learn to sword-fight in bars. There is something very *wrong* about you, and I'm going to find out what it is."

The deep thrum of incubus power felt overwhelming here, and I glanced at the violet magic pulsing between his fingers. What *was* that?

Right about now, I was wishing I'd armed myself with more than just the misericorde dagger. With a sword, I was pretty sure I could take on all three of them at once. But I could always jump—

Maddan took another step closer, and I surged with desire. What the hell? I felt like the incubi were all around me

"Have you heard of distillation?" asked Maddan, taking a step closer. "I refer to the distillation of magic, of course. It's something the noble Mor learn from a young age. But of course, you're not one of us."

Then, he hurled that ball of violet magic at me, and warmth spread through my chest.

CHAPTER 24

*J*couldn't quite focus on his words, because wild heat was building in my body, a ferocious need that made me want to run into the streets and hunt down Ruadan.

"'I've distilled incubus magic," Maddan went on. The barguest and Sea Monster flanked him. "I want to know your secrets, and this should get you to loosen up a little."

I had a vague sense that I needed to attack him, but I just couldn't think clearly. My legs were trembling with a raw, animal need.

In the next moment, Maddan's wet hand was around my throat, his face pressed down close to mine.

"Tell me your secrets, gutter fae, while I use you like I used the others of your kind."

Despite my disgust, a wave of aching need washed over me. He picked up my wrist—the one holding the dagger—and slammed it into the wall. Even as I knew he was hurting me, waves of pleasure washed through me at the force.

He was hiking up my dress, pressing me against the cold wood as I scrambled to remember what I was doing here, what my name was … anything at all. I dropped whatever was in my hand.

"Tell me where you come from," said Maddan. He ripped the lumen crystal from my neck, shoving it into his pocket.

As I stared into the calculating eyes of the fae prince, clarity came slamming back into me. Since the bastard had stolen my lumen crystal, I could no longer simply jump away.

I brought my knee up hard into his groin, and he doubled over. Then, I gripped his hair, bringing his head down hard onto my knee. Sea Monster lunged for me, and I smashed my elbow into his jaw with the full force of my strength.

So much for moving in the shadows. Any second now, the incubi were about to realize there were a bunch of fae brawling in one of their corridors, and that bodies littered their fuck den. But I was being attacked, three on one, and I had to neutralize these arseholes before I could get out of here.

The barguest growled, and I kicked him hard in the chest. He stumbled back into Sea Monster.

Crush your enemies completely.

At this point, I wanted them all dead. Savus had never instructed us not to kill the other novices, and I suspected he encouraged it.

Bloodlust surged—dark and hungry. I wanted the bodies of fallen fae lying at my feet once more, just like that day in the arena....

When Sea Monster swung for me, I ducked, then punched him in the crotch. He doubled over. As he did, I slammed my elbow into his kidney.

Lightning-fast, I clamped my hands hard on his head, and I twisted. The sharp crack of bone told me I'd snapped his neck, though only iron would kill him for good. A dark smile curled my lips. Death—this was what I was born for.

I whirled to take out Maddan. I hammered him with blows, one after another, bloodying his face, cracking his nose.

I was just starting to gain control of the fight when something pierced my ribs, cold as a glacier. The barguest had stabbed me.

A wave of dread pulled me under.

I looked down with horror at the reaping dagger jutting from my ribs. Emptiness pooled in my chest, a gnawing, glacial magic. I started shaking violently, my veins filling with ice.

And yet ... I hadn't been sent to the shadow hell, yet. Why not? What in the seven hells was happening?

The two remaining shadow fae stared at me. I could no longer control my body, couldn't lift my fist to punch them. Shivering convulsed me, and I hugged myself.

The two fae males gaped at me as my skin frosted over. I needed my lumen stone back.

The barguest bared his canines. "Why is she still here?"

"She should be in the shadow hell," Maddan spat, purple magic still flickering at his fingertips. "I told you there was something very wrong with her. Even the void is rejecting her."

I mastered enough control over my shaking hand to bring it to the dagger's hilt, and I pulled the blade out of me. But my teeth wouldn't stop chattering, and the coldness was spreading.

When I'd been with Ruadan in the park, he'd counteracted the iciness of the shadow magic with incubus lust.

What I needed was another hit of incubus magic to warm me up before I froze to death. Through chattering teeth, I managed, "You were so convinced you could seduce my secrets out of me. And yet even with incubus magic at your fingertips, you revolt me."

Rage flashed across Maddan's features, and he threw the ball of magic at me. It slammed into my chest. Now, warmth spread through my ribs and deep into my core, melting the intense chill of the shadow magic. Even as I shivered, desire started to blossom in my mind, and I thought of Ruadan kissing me.

As the barguest took a step closer, I felt my back arching, my eyes going dazed. I was trembling with need—but I was no longer freezing to death. For just a moment, I leaned back against a door, closing my eyes. The combination of shadow magic and desire dizzied me.

One of the fae males was yanking off my skirt, and I felt the cold whisper of air slipping over my skin.

I lifted my hands to push him away, mustering up just enough strength to punch him in the throat. It wasn't a hard punch, but I landed it squarely on his Adam's apple. He staggered back, snarling.

Then, a blur of black behind him, and the scent of pine….

I stared as Ruadan clamped his hands on the barguest's head. A glacial fury burned in Ruadan's dark eyes, his lip curled to expose his canines.

He didn't simply snap the barguest's neck. No, Ruadan clamped one arm around Dog Boy's jaw, the other around his shoulders, and he *tore.* He ripped the barguest's head right off. Blood sprayed all over the floor. Not the most discreet way to kill a man, but it looked like wrath had consumed him.

With a burst of shadows, Maddan shadow-jumped away.

Ruadan pulled an iron sword from his sheath, and he brought it down into the barguest's body. Then, he severed Sea Monster's head.

Both dead.

Tremors wracked me, a combination of the dagger's freezing magic and the distilled lust that still pulsed through my core.

I was trying desperately to focus while completely distracted by the feel of my silk shirt sliding against my bare breasts. My fingertips trailed down the front of my chest, and Ruadan's eyes watched the movement.

Ruadan rushed over to me, grabbing me around the waist so I didn't fall. I breathed in his masculine scent, and heat radiated from his body. Some part of me wanted to show him how much I ached for him, and my fingertips were inching their way into my knickers.

He lifted my chin to look into my eyes, demanding answers, and I blinked to clear my mind.

"Right." I leaned into his powerful chest, whispering, "The dagger. Maddan stabbed me with the reaping dagger. And they hit me with distilled incubus magic. They took my lumen crystal." I clutched at the fabric of Ruadan's shirt, trying to remain upright as my knees buckled. "Can you shadow-jump with me in your arms?"

He shook his head.

Shit. We'd have to get out of here the old-fashioned way. Walking. Except, I couldn't walk.

Ruadan gripped my waist, and the feel of his hands on me sent molten heat racing through my blood. Since he was an incubus, my desire was distracting him, too. His violet eyes were darkening to black, his animal side taking over. He snarled, his fingers gripping me harder, and he pushed me against the wood of the door behind me. I cupped his face, looking up into his eyes.

Then, a woman's scream ripped through the nightclub, and fear raked its claws into my chest.

We'd been discovered.

CHAPTER 25

A powerful force impacted Ruadan from behind —once, twice. My gaze flicked over his shoulder, and my heart sputtered. The incubi really *were* masters of shadow-leaping, and one of them was looming over Ruadan right now, leathery wings spread. His form had shifted, and talons now sprouted where his hands should be.

When Ruadan turned to face him, I caught a glimpse of the deep gashes carved into his shoulder.

"Eight fallen friends," hissed the incubus. "The work of the spell-slayers. You're one of us. Are you so disloyal to your kind?"

Ruadan drew his sword. In a blur of motion, he carved it through the incubus's shoulder, severing his body from collarbone to waist.

That's a hell of a sword.

But after the blow, Ruadan's body slumped. The

wound gaped in his back, blood pouring out at an alarming rate.

Ruadan whirled, and his fae ears twitched. He sniffed the air. The scent of incubi hung heavily around us. Depending on how many we'd left alive, we could be just a few minutes from death.

Dizzying shadow and lust magic curled around my ribs, making my knees weak, and I slumped to the floor. Neither Ruadan or I were in great fighting form, now.

With a grunt, Ruadan scooped me up, and I wrapped my arms around his neck. He pulled open one of the doors, rushing me inside.

It wasn't even a full room—little more than a narrow booth. Thin chinks of light streamed inside flecking a wooden bench with the golden candlelight from outside. Ruadan sat, cradling me in his arms.

Despite the lust blazing from my body, the incubi probably had no idea how to pinpoint where I was, considering the entire joint was full of naked females writhing in ecstasy.

Ruadan frowned, lifting the hem of my shirt a little, and the brush of his fingertips sent a rush of hot tingles. It took me a moment to realize he was looking for the place where I'd been stabbed. Blood streamed from my wound, but it was a thin puncture, and it apparently hadn't pierced anything crucial. His forehead wrinkled.

"I know what you're thinking," I whispered, trying

to fight my body's shuddering. "How does someone get stabbed with a reaping dagger and survive?"

His eyes met mine, and he nodded once.

"I have no idea." Ruadan's powerful energy rushed over my bare legs. "And I'm a little distracted right now."

He traced his fingertips over the wound, and his magic curled around it. Shadowy tendrils sank into my flesh, and I stared as the wound began healing over right before my eyes. The magic curled over my abdomen, smoothing my skin.

He met my gaze expectantly.

Right now, I felt acutely aware of every point of contact between our bodies, of his fingers on my upper thigh, of how close my mouth was to his neck. His primal magic charged the air. I could imagine him slipping his hands into my knickers, cupping between my legs while I writhed against him. I realized my own hand had crept into the hem of my knickers, and I flushed, yanking it out again.

Ruadan's posture was rigid, the unflinching gaze of a true soldier. And yet his eyes held that animal darkness.

I leaned in closer to Ruadan, whispering in his ear. "Is the plan to wait it out until the incubi are gone from this corridor?" I felt compelled to give his ear a nip, and his body tensed.

He nodded, still staring straight ahead.

It was a stupid plan. Incubi like Ruadan healed through sexual contact. I could be healing him right now. His body instinctively knew that, and he was practically glowing with pale, violet magic, already feeding off my desire. Even as he stared straight ahead, his arms tightened around me. One fingertip found its way to the hollow of my hip, stroking in lazy circles.

Then, he met my gaze, and the intensity of his dark eyes took me apart. Those slow, lazy circles on my hip made my breath hitch.

In his arms, breathing in the scent of his magic, a deep ache built within me—a wild, unfulfilled need, so powerful I wanted to beg him to ease it.

His attention was completely locked on me as he teased my hipbone, stirring my lust. A slow, pleasurable torture that left me panting. *More.*

I hooked my leg over him, sliding over his body so that I straddled him, and he stared into my eyes. Just minutes ago, I'd been freezing to death. Now, I felt as if warm honey were pooling in my body.

Seeming to lose control of himself, he snarled and clenched hard on my waist with one hand. His other slid up my back, the intense pressure making my spine arch against his palm. When his hand reached the shoulder of my silk shirt, he pulled it down, exposing my peaked breast. He leaned in to kiss me, his tongue flicking against mine. As his thumb brushed over my nipple, I moved my hips over him. Our kiss intensified, and I lost all sense of time and place.

Then, with a swift and rough movement, he lifted me up, pressing me hard against the wooden wall. My bare legs wrapped tightly around his waist. He pinned me to the wall, his gaze penetrating me.

I raked my fingernails down his back, wild animal need overtaking me. I couldn't remember how words worked anymore.

Already, I'd fed him more than enough lust to heal. But I wasn't done. I needed him to soothe my own ache. An electrical current was passing between us, and I was drawing strength from it, filling the empty void of the shadow magic. He leaned in, kissing me hungrily. He crushed his mouth against mine with all the wild desperation of a last kiss.

I groaned into his mouth, threading my fingers into his hair.

His hand slipped into my knickers. I tilted back my head, writhing against him, moaning louder.

Then, he clamped a hand over my mouth, and I caught my breath. My mind snapped back into place.

Right. The incubi. I was getting too loud.

He pulled his hand from my mouth, then gave one last, heated kiss to my neck. But his muscles had tensed completely as he remembered the threat outside.

Slowly, his eyes shifted back to violet.

He lowered me to the ground and put a finger over his lips. My body slid against his, unfulfilled need ripping my mind apart. But even through my fog of desire I could understand that perhaps, in the middle of a battle with incubi, we had more important things to do than banging in a closet. Like, surviving.

Ruadan pulled a piece of paper out of his pocket and began writing.

Can you walk?

I could. In fact, Ruadan had filled me with so much of his magic that I felt ready to tear into a whole horde of incubi.

I pulled him close to whisper, "I just need my weapon back."

He pushed the door open an inch, peering out. Then, he grabbed me by the hand, and we slipped into the dark corridor. I snatched my dagger from the floor where I'd dropped it.

Shadows lashed the air around Ruadan, billowing until they ensconced us in darkness. His magic would help disguise us as we crept out of the nightclub.

At the end of the corridor, Ruadan pushed through an oak door into a dark stairwell, and we crept down the creaking stairs.

When we reached the bottom floor, the electrical smell of the incubi hit me like a wave. We'd emerged into a smoky room, one filled with glowing violet lights, ornate rugs, and silky pillows. It wasn't empty, but it seemed to be mostly naked women, who didn't notice us. They were too busy tending to themselves.

At least—until a ginger woman with extremely perky breasts pointed at Ruadan, a smile curling her lips. "This one is different. This one looks like a god. I want *him*."

An inexplicable sense of possessiveness snapped

through me, and I nearly punched her. But Ruadan gripped my hand harder, pulling me toward the door.

Just before we reached it, a hissing noise turned my head. From behind, six incubi were closing in on us, brandishing swords and talons.

I needed to get one of their swords to even out the odds.

Already, Ruadan's sword was clashing with an incubus's. I locked my sights on one of the incubi—a blond demon closest to me—and hurled the blood-soaked reaping dagger. It landed in his chest. When he collapsed, I darted, snatching his sword from his limp hand.

I whirled, and my new sword clashed against a demon's.

Ruadan's magic filled me, imbuing me with strength. Now, I moved like a night wind: fast, silent, and cold. Ruadan cut his sword through another incubus, slicing him at the waist.

Two down, four to go.

I fought desperately, whirling and ducking as I parried the attacks of the incubi around me. Ruadan hacked through another demon. I grunted, just barely managing to fend them off as the fight wore on.

As I fought, blocking blow after blow, Ruadan's magic began to wear off. The reaping dagger hadn't sent me to hell, and yet I could feel the shadow hell living within me, blooming like a disease. My veins were icing over. I swung more wildly, just barely catching an incubus in the side.

From behind, pain sliced through my arm as an incubus ripped into it. Another lash of his talons ripped through my shoulder, tearing my flesh.

Ruadan pivoted, slicing his sword in a sharp arc through the incubus's neck. He picked up speed, a whirl of motion now.

I staggered back as iciness ripped through my bones. Shivering wildly, I collapsed onto the rug. Pain splintered my torso.

I *hated* being weak, but I couldn't fight the rising void within me. At least I wasn't in hell.

Yet.

I stared at Ruadan—a tornado of steel and dark magic, cutting into the incubi.

Glaciers were moving within my blood, and I couldn't keep my eyes open any longer. Arctic darkness enveloped me.

CHAPTER 26

I woke to something completely unfamiliar, so startling I nearly screamed. Pillows, a mattress, a blanket.

Late afternoon light slanted into the room through diamond-paned windows.

When I breathed in, scenting pine, I knew I was in Ruadan's bed. I was still freezing, shaking hard, and my teeth chattered violently.

For the first time, I noticed another scent on him. Not pine, and not shadow magic. *Apples.* I loved that smell.

A powerful arm hooked around me, pulling me close to bare skin. A strand of white-blonde hair draped over my shoulder. I glanced behind me.

Ruadan was trying to warm me, and heat radiated from his body into mine. I was pretty sure he was also using a low dose of that incubus magic to counteract the shadows. I nestled into him.

I ran my hand over my shoulder where the incubus had attacked me with his talons. Already, the skin had smoothed over. Ruadan had healed me. Now, his magic skimmed over my skin, caressing me. He was using just enough incubus magic to keep the void from consuming me from the inside out. Warm honey swept through my core as his magic pulsed around me, and I had to restrain myself from rolling over and kissing him.

I closed my eyes, drifting off to sleep, and I dreamt I was back at the incubi's nest, back in that booth with Ruadan. His hand was fisted into my hair, tilting my head back, and his body pressed against mine. The night air and lust magic whispered over my bare legs, raising goosebumps.

He reached for my knickers, pulling them down. He spun me around so I faced the wall—

I woke to the sound of Ruadan groaning. Apparently, in my sleep, I'd pulled off my clothes. Even worse, I'd hooked my leg over him, and I may have been slightly rubbing against him. His own body was completely rigid, jaw clenched, with that "good soldier" look on his face like he was enduring something appalling.

Still, his fingers were clamped on my waist, and he wasn't pushing me away. In fact, his grip was growing tighter, almost pulling me closer. He was just ... resisting.

I couldn't quite bring myself to unlock my body from his.

"I need to get out of here," I said. With a jolt, I realized I hadn't made any progress on finding the key.

Unless....

I glanced at his bare chest, and my pulse started racing. There, on his sternum, a fae rune glowed with silver light. My heart began to race. The key was part of his body.

I sucked in a sharp breath, and dread coiled through me. If that was the key, I might as well give up now, because I would not be hauling Ruadan's entire body to Baleros.

Shit. Shit. Shit.

I felt like I'd been punched in the gut. I pulled away from Ruadan, sitting up straight, the drafty air kissing my bare skin.

As soon as I moved away from Ruadan, I felt as if the void were ripping me apart from the inside out, and ice shuddered through me. My vision began darkening. I hadn't been sent to the void, but I hadn't escaped the effects of the dagger, either.

"I can't stay here." I mumbled. "I have to get out of here." I had to get to Ciara. Maybe I could just kill Baleros. Frigid magic iced my blood, and my teeth chattered.

Ruadan reached for me, pulling me in close until his warmth enveloped me. My breathing slowed again, my heartbeat calming. And as I drifted off, I started dreaming of the booth again, of hard kisses and arching backs....

* * *

THE COLD WOKE ME AGAIN, a bone-deep chill that had me scrambling to wrap myself in blankets. Through a darkening haze, I stared at Ruadan across the room. Thin slivers of moonlight streamed over the flagstones, and candles guttered in sconces, casting wavering light over Ruadan's bare chest.

Shivering, I stared at the glowing mark on his chest. I pulled the blankets more tightly around me, watching as Ruadan touched his tattoo. It glowed with a pale, silvery light, like starlight. Darkness spilled out from his body.

Shadows writhed around the room, then gathered over a spot in the flagstone floor. The tendrils of darkness whirled in wild eddies, until at last, the stones opened up and gave way to dark, glistening water. A portal of midnight waters flecked with starlight.

Ice slid through me. It *was* the key on his chest, and it was a part of him. Cold panic coiled around my heart. There was no way out of this.

I stared as a dark pool of water opened in the floor, its rippled surface glinting. The void gaped deeper in my chest, and I pulled the blanket around myself to cover my bare breasts. I had no idea where my clothes were at this point—probably crammed deep in the blankets. It seemed as though I couldn't bring myself to keep them on when I was around Ruadan and his particular brand of magic.

In any case, if Bael was about to come stark naked out of the water, he could hardly criticize my attire.

The cold was making my muscles seize up. Not just the cold, but that gnawing void, the painful emptiness....

I clenched my jaw, focusing on the World Key. I'd found it—what I'd been looking for all along. The only way to get it off Ruadan would be to kill him and cut it off him.

The void opened a bit larger in my chest, an emptiness so expansive it seemed like it was going to swallow me whole.

I have to kill Ruadan.

Dark shadows whipped about him, slicing through the air around his body. He'd let down his guard, and he seemed to trust me now. He'd let me into his bed, taken his shirt off in front of me. He was no longer hiding the World Key from me, as if I could be trusted.... He clearly didn't know me at all.

Baleros had turned me rotten through and through. Baleros had taught me to strike as soon as the enemy lowered his defenses. I could kill him in bed, take the skin from his chest—

Emptiness cut through me so sharply I thought I might die.

I stared as a beautiful man crawled out of the pool, his body dripping with water. His silver eyes had the cold sheen of moonlight, and dark curls framed his face.

The cold was making me convulse, and I fell back on the bed.

In another instant, Ruadan was by my side, scooping me into his lap. His magic stroked my skin, a velvety touch that warmed me. Had it been just a moment ago I'd been imagining how I'd kill him? Because right now, I was hugging him and leaning into his chest to breathe in the scent of pine. To say I felt conflicted was the understatement of the fucking year.

The silver-eyed one hovered over me, staring down with curiosity.

"Who are you?" I asked through chattering teeth.

"Caine." He looked at Ruadan. "You're telling me that someone stabbed her with a reaping dagger? One belonging to Nyxobas?"

How the fuck were they communicating? Ruadan wasn't speaking.

"And she's still alive?" Caine continued, incredulous. "What in the seven hells is she?"

If my nudity bothered him, he didn't show it. When I glimpsed the faint ghost of phantom wings behind him, I had the sense that he might be part incubus, too.

"All right," said Caine. "It seems as if part of the void is inside her. We can try to pull it out and absorb it. You'll need to send it back into the shadow realm using the World Key."

I was trying to tune into his words, although most of my thoughts were intensely focused on every place where Ruadan's body touched mine. His bare chest was heating my naked body, and I stared at the glowing fae rune at his throat.

I was having a hard time concentrating on anything except Ruadan's arms curling around me. It made it hard for me to think straight, and I wanted my mind back so I could start killing things again, like I was born to do.

But I could feel a wild, dark power trembling over my skin. The two gorgeous half-incubi closed their eyes. Now, the candles flickered in their sconces until they snuffed out, and the moonlight in the room began to dim. A thin frost spread over the stone floor, the bed —everything in the room but us. Glimmering shadows spilled from my body and whirled into Caine and Ruadan.

Even though cold seemed to be spreading within the room, my own body grew warmer. I closed my eyes, my mind whirling with cosmic visions—the birth of stars, the spinning of galaxies. A black hole, sucking in light. When I opened my eyes again, it looked to me as if the shadows in the room were breathing, like a bellows rhythmically expanding and contracting. My own breath moved in tune to the pulsing of the shadows.

In the darkness, in the hollow void of my chest, embers began to smolder, warming my ribs. I fell back into Ruadan's arms, closing my eyes, and I breathed in the scent of pine.

CHAPTER 27

 hen I opened my eyes again, Ruadan had left. I sat up, letting the sheets fall off me, until I noticed the shadows writhing in the corner of the room. A pair of silver eyes glowed from the darkness.

Once my eyes adjusted to the whorls of dark magic, I realized that Caine was sitting in the corner, drinking straight out of my whiskey bottle. A raven sat on his shoulder, its head cocked. Caine's clothes and hair were still damp from the portal.

The pool of starlit water still glimmered in the center of the room.

Caine sipped my whiskey. If he weren't so shockingly good-looking, the whole "lurking in the shadows, drinking whiskey while a naked woman sleeps" situation would be beyond creepy, but pretty blokes could get away with anything.

I snatched the sheets up, covering my breasts, but he didn't seem too bothered either way.

"You're still here," I said.

"Very observant. Ruadan did tell me you were clever, and you're not proving him wrong so far."

I arched an eyebrow. "He talks to you?"

"Not in words."

"Right. Of course. That makes total sense." I had no idea what he was talking about. It took me a moment to realize that I had now completely recovered from the reaping dagger. I no longer felt cold, or consumed with desire. "How did you fix me? How did you pull the shadow void from me?"

"The shadow void is already part of Ruadan and me. With our combined power, we were able to draw it into our bodies and absorb it. It doesn't hurt us."

I blinked. "What do you mean it's already part of you?"

Caine took another sip of my whiskey. "Nyxobas is our grandfather."

"Your grandfather is the god of night and shadows."

"Hence, Ruadan and I are demigods of the night."

I arched an eyebrow. "Wouldn't that make you a quarter—"

"Still considered demigods."

"Sure you are."

Caine narrowed his silver eyes, clearly irritated.

"So, what—you're brothers?" I asked.

"Half-brothers. He's even older than I am. I never knew he existed until after our father died."

"I'm sorry about your dad."

"Don't be. Our father deserved his death." Caine rose and slid the whiskey bottle across the stone table. "Thanks for the drink. My brother asked me to talk to you about something before I return to my realm."

"What?"

"The fae who tried to kill you still lives in this fortress."

Anger roiled in my chest. "Maddan? He should have been sent home in disgrace for fucking up our mission."

A slow shrug from Caine. "Grand Master Savus wouldn't allow it. He values ruthlessness, which is why you're here, as I understand it. And more importantly, the prince's father has been donating millions to the Institute." Caine held up a glowing, violet lumen crystal. "But while Ruadan was beating the living shit out of the fae boy, he pulled this off him. It should make it easier to defend yourself if he returns."

"Where is Ruadan?" I asked.

"Still petitioning Grand Master Savus for permission to execute the fae prince."

"Why does he want to execute him so badly?" Was he protective of me, or—?

"I think he just likes executing novices, to be honest. Particularly the rule-breaking kind."

"Of course. The Shadow Fae value ruthlessness." I let out a long, slow breath. Right. *Don't let this situation mess with your head, Arianna.* He wasn't trying to protect me. He just … liked executing novices.

Baleros's seventh law of power: Kill, or be killed.

There was no way out of the Institute without breaking several rules. I was going to end up on Ruadan's kill list, one way or another.

My chest tightened. Unless I took him out first.

Caine's eyes pierced me to the bone. "What are you? Why didn't the blade send you to the void?"

I shook my head. "I have no idea. I never knew my parents."

He stared at me for an uncomfortably long time. "You aren't as good a liar as you think you are."

My breath caught in my throat. Caine was starting to get under my skin. "You and your brother are both deeply unnerving, do you know that?"

"I have a charming side. Ruadan does not, as you might have noticed. Silently brooding, disapproving of alcohol, updating his kill list, executing people…. Those are his favorite pastimes."

"Mmm. Don't take this the wrong way, but I'd say you've kept your charming side well-hidden so far."

"You're not wearing any clothes. The effect of my charm would be overwhelming. Like a human learning the true names of the gods."

"Right." Gods below. The ego on this guy.

I took the lumen crystal from him, staring at the violet glow. It almost seemed like Ruadan cared about keeping me safe, but I knew better than to trust gestures of kindness. I had to find a way to kill him.

Even though the two incubi had pulled the void out of my body, coldness still washed through me.

When I looked up again, Caine was already crossing back to the portal. The raven fluttered off his shoulder and flew out the open window. Caine leapt into the water.

I shivered as Baleros's voice whispered in the darkest depths of my skull. *Neutralize all threats as quickly and efficiently as possible.*

Ruadan might be a demigod, but he'd let down his guard around me. He didn't see me as a threat, but that didn't mean he cared about me or anything ridiculous like that. It just meant he'd gotten sloppy while he waited to execute me. And tonight, while he slept in his comfortable bed, I had a threat to neutralize.

I STILL HAD HALF a bottle of whiskey left, and now was as good a time as any to drink it. I finally pulled on some clothes, and I sat by the cold, stone table. Night had begun to fall, and Ruadan hadn't yet returned.

I clasped the lumen crystal around my throat, and shadow magic shot through my blood. But now—after everything I'd endured with the reaping dagger—I could handle it easily.

My stomach rumbled, and I rifled through my bag for one of my lollipops. Somewhere, beneath the duct tape, flashlights, and bandages, I found an old protein bar, only partially eaten. I delved into it, ignoring its staleness.

I had to keep my energy up for tonight. You couldn't assassinate a demigod on an empty stomach. Not one of Baleros's laws, but it seemed like a good rule to live by.

I scanned the wall, my gaze roaming over Ruadan's collection of blades. I tried to push out the rising cold in my chest, that corrosive sense of emptiness. The voice in my head telling me not to do it.

Crush your enemies completely.

I needed two blades—one silver, to cut the tracking mark off the back of my neck. The other, iron, to drive into Ruadan's body when he slept. Either could be used to cut the World Key off him.

I hugged myself, shivering. Why did it feel as if the void hadn't completely left me?

A knock on the door pulled me out of my dark thoughts, and I whirled. I wasn't ready to face Ruadan yet, or look him in the eyes. My body tense, I crossed to the door and pulled it open.

Melusine stood beside Aengus. She was gripping a paper bag.

I exhaled a shaky breath as I looked at her. "Good. You're alive. So you have that advantage over two of our fellow novices."

Aengus leaned against the door frame. "What are you?"

I crossed my arms. "Alive. That's all that matters."

"What in the seven hells happened in there?" he asked. "Why did the others attack you? We were watching it all through a scrying mirror, but it was hard to see anything through the darkness."

Melusine tapped her fingernails on the doorframe. "He's been interrogating me, but I didn't see anything. I was too busy reaping."

My fingers clenched into fists. I was in here trying to plan a murder, and I didn't want to rehash our giant novice fuck-up. "Maddan and the others couldn't get into the club at first," I said. "They'd thought it would be an easy trial for them, that the ladies would be all hepped up on incubus magic and unable to think clearly. When they finally got inside and found that the girls were embarrassing them, they wanted to teach me a lesson. They were pissed I'd killed the king in our last trial, and they seemed to think I have some shady past —which, surprise, I do. After all, I'm just a gutter fae. But I know a knob-end when I see one, and the truth is, Maddan is no better than the bar-brawling demons who flip over tables every time they think they've been slighted by a chick. Rage rules their minds. Turned out, they were the ones who couldn't think clearly."

Baleros's fifth law of power: Don't let your emotions govern your decisions.

"But they're dead now," I went on. "All except Maddan."

"Idiots," spat Aengus.

Melusine thrust the paper bag at me. "You missed dinner. I brought you a steak pie."

I fought the urge to hug her. I didn't want to alert

them that I might be on my way out of here soon. Instead, I just smiled. "Thanks, Melusine."

"See you at the trial tomorrow."

I nodded. I hadn't even known there was a trial tomorrow, but it wasn't like I needed to prepare. I'd be long gone by the time the sun rose—with Ruadan's blood on my hands.

CHAPTER 28

I lay curled up on the stone floor by Ruadan's bed, pretending to sleep. No blanket. No pillows.

I felt ice-cold, inside and out.

It must have been around midnight by the time he returned.

When he snatched the blanket off his bed to cover me with it, my breath caught in my chest. For just a brief moment, warmth sparked in my chest, my glacial resolve cracking....

Then, I extinguished it again. Like everyone said. I was ruthless. And the blanket was just another gods-damned butterscotch sweet.

I wasn't going to let my emotions rule me. I watched through a slit in my eyes as Ruadan pulled off his shirt. I swallowed hard, my gaze roaming over his perfect body. I practically sighed. What a waste of a beautiful man. I wished it could have been different. I wished I'd gotten to hear him speak, to learn his secrets....

Kill, or be killed.

I watched as he crawled into bed, my body seeming to grow colder as I contemplated what was coming next. For what seemed like ages, Ruadan lay in bed, staring up at the ceiling. His muscles looked tense, just as he had when I'd shared a bed with him.

At last, his eyes closed. I waited until his chest slowly rose and fell. The dark pulsing of shadows that always surrounded him began to ebb, as if they, too, were falling asleep.

Silently, I reached underneath my body, where I'd hidden two blades. I had to act quickly. Every extra second was another second he could wake up and discover me.

I rose, my chest aching with a yawning emptiness.

This was it. This was who I was. A ruthless killer, but a survivor. Baleros might have been the worst person I'd ever met, but he'd taught me how to stay alive.

The lumen crystal glowed over my sternum, and I shadow-jumped. I landed on top of Ruadan, my arm raised, gripping the knife—

His violet eyes opened, and time seemed to slow down. I was hesitating, and hesitation meant death.

I twirled the knife and started to bring the hilt down hard—I could knock him out, then decide.

But as my hand descended, he caught my wrist. He snarled, baring his canines.

In a blur of night magic, he flipped me over, pinning me to the bed. The move took my breath away, and I stared up into his darkening eyes.

His animalistic side was coming out. If I didn't get out of this, I'd become executed novice number three within the next few moments.

Inwardly, I cursed myself for hesitating. I should have just stabbed him.

Was he hesitating, too? I wasn't going to wait around to find out. I thrust my hips upward, knocking him off balance, and I rolled, yanking one of my wrists free.

I didn't hesitate this time. Just as it had so many times before, a desperate, wild will to live consumed me. I slammed my fist again and again into Ruadan's face. Then, I snatched the silver blade off the bed.

I brought it down hard into his chest, piercing his heart.

Blood poured from the wound. I'd stopped his heart completely, and he wouldn't be getting up anytime soon. But as soon as someone pulled the weapon out, he'd start to recover.

I was shaking, trembling with the cold, and for just a moment, tears pierced my eyes. Panic was ripping through my mind. I'd failed.

I'd used the silver blade. Not iron. He'd have a hell of a hangover, but he'd live.

Apparently, I'd gone soft since he started giving me blankets and pillows, and I couldn't bring myself to end him. The first thing he'd do when he woke up would be to hunt me down and yet....

The fucking blanket. That stupid fucking blanket.

I was letting my emotions rule me, and it was a problem.

A hot tear spilled down my cheek, and I wiped it off with the back of my hand. I hated myself right now, my inability to do what needed to be done.

I started pacing the room, my mind racing.

Hesitation is death.

I hated Baleros with every fiber of my being, but his teachings had been my salvation. Without them, I'd be dead now.

Get in your enemy's head. Knowledge gives you power over a person.

And yet....

The fucker had become so deeply embedded in my head that I sometimes couldn't figure out where his ideas ended and mine began. Almost as if our minds had melded.

And that meant I knew how he thought, too.

Confuse your enemy by utilizing the unexpected.

My fingernails were piercing my palm, drawing blood, as I frantically tried to think of a way out of this.

Baleros claimed he had eyes within the Institute— that if I betrayed him, he'd kill Ciara. But that was just the kind of bullshit Baleros *would* say. If he truly had forces working for him here, then why didn't he know what the key was in the first place? If he'd known already it was a part of Ruadan's body, he would have sent me on a kill mission. He hadn't. He'd sent me to steal.

Of course Baleros had lied, because that's what he did.

I clenched my jaw tight. What if I could kill Baleros and save Ciara?

I had to find him first, but if I knew how he thought, I might be able to puzzle it out.

I glanced at Ruadan's body, relieved to find he wasn't moving.

What did Baleros believe about himself? He viewed himself as a sort of god among monsters. That was what he used to call us gladiators—the monsters. He liked to drive that word into us, until I'd believed it myself. Maybe I still believed it. Maybe that's why I'd just driven a knife into the chest of my new mentor.

Baleros had studied us, manipulating us all the time like a puppet master. But we scared him, too. There was some dead philosopher he used to quote. Something like "whoever fights monsters needs to watch out that he doesn't become a monster, too." Then something like, "When you gaze too long into the abyss, the abyss gazes back at you…."

"Well, fucker," I said out loud. "I'm gazing back at you. I know how you think."

Baleros's eighteenth law of power: When you achieve greatness, cling onto it with all your strength.

Baleros had thrived during the anarchic period between the apocalypse and the reconstruction. Practically singlehandedly, he'd rebuilt the old Roman gladiatorial ring under London's city streets. He'd employed a legion of slave masters, each of them making money off their fighters, but he'd pulled all the strings behind the scenes.

The Shadow Fae and the reconstruction ruined all that for him. All the gladiators—except me—were sent into the supernatural realms.

If I closed my eyes, I could envision Baleros, haunting the old amphitheater, looking regal and shabby at the same time. He'd mentally relive his glory days, when the monsters had treated him like the emperor he was supposed to be. Baleros had adopted the old Roman ways, encouraging his veneration. Within those stone walls, he felt not just like an emperor, but like a god.

I touched the lumen crystal at my throat.

I could shadow-jump, now. Baleros couldn't do that. I could take him.

I glanced at Ruadan again, my whole body trembling. His body was still as a grave. He looked completely dead, even though I knew he wasn't. Perhaps I could have convinced him to come with me if I hadn't stabbed him in the chest. But that would be a risk, too. Ruadan would be going on a kill mission. I was going on a rescue mission. Totally different objectives.

My mind whirled frantically, and I felt like I was coming undone. I willed my heart to slow down.

My plan was to get Ciara out of Baleros's clutches—ideally, to kill him, as well, but Ciara's rescue was the priority. Then, we'd have to flee London. Both of us would be living like fugitives, hiding from the Shadow Fae for the rest of our lives. There was no way out of that. We'd just have to get used to it, and eventually, maybe the Shadow Fae would forget about us.

Whatever the case, I had to get the fuck out of here, now. I honestly had no idea how long a demigod would stay down for. It wasn't like I'd fought them in the arena.

I was still shaking when I crossed to Ruadan's wall, and I pulled another knife from his arsenal. A silver blade, just like the one in his chest. But I had a different purpose for this one.

I brought it to the nape of my neck, where Ruadan had marked me with the tracking spell days ago.

Wincing, I carved the blade into my skin. I gritted my teeth as the pain speared my neck. Melusine would probably have a magical way to handle this, but all I had was brute force on my side.

At last, I'd cut it off. Blood dripped down my fingers, pooling on the floor.

If I didn't staunch the bleeding, Ruadan would be able to track me within moments of waking. Situations like this were exactly why I carried the bug-out bag with me. You never knew when you'd have to carve magical tattoos off your body. I pulled out a bottle of water, gauze, and my other medical supplies, and I washed the blood from my hands. I spread some antiseptic on the wound, grunting as it stung the open flesh. Then, I taped it tightly with thick layers of gauze. And one more layer of duct tape, for good measure.

When that was cleaned up, I pulled off my bloodied shirt, crumpling it in a ball. I pulled on a fresh black shirt.

Suitably cleaned up, I snatched a piece of paper out of my bag, along with a pen, and I hastily scrawled:

SORRY FOR STABBING YOU.

Then,

THANKS FOR THE BLANKET.

I cringed. That sounded sarcastic, like I was taunting him, but I actually meant it.

"Fucking butterscotch sweets," I grumbled, aware that I was sounding increasingly like a lunatic with every minute that passed.

In any case, writing pretty things wasn't my strength, and I didn't have time to obsess over the exact phrasing. I left the note by his side for when he woke up.

I crossed back to his arsenal, selecting the finest-looking sheath, and I tightened it around my waist. I picked up the iron knife from his bed and carefully slid it into the sheath. Even Baleros had a weakness. And as a fae, that weakness was iron.

I crossed to one of the windows and lifted it until the chilly night air spilled into the room. Shadows claimed the courtyard. Perfect for jumping.

I was pretty sure the halls were lined with magic that could track our every movement, and maybe it would set off alarms. Keeping to the Tower Green was safer. And with the lumen stone, I might be able to get out of here before any of the Shadow Fae got a chance to react.

Ruadan was the only incubus in here, the only one who could naturally shadow-jump. And I'd laid him out cold with his own silver knife. A twinge of guilt flickered through me, but I shoved it away again.

Glacial night magic whispered over my skin, surging in my blood. I gripped the straps of my bug-out bag. Living in a castle had been nice, but it was time for me to take my leave before someone killed me. I sucked in a shaky breath, stared down at a far corner of the courtyard, and I jumped.

CHAPTER 29

I moved like a lunar wind, jumping along the dark, cobbled alleys of the Tower. No bells rang, no alarms as I reached the final, outer wall. Thank fuck for that, because the gates were locked, and shadow-leaping wouldn't get me through them.

I scaled the rough stone wall, finding footholds and handholds in the jagged stones until I reached the top. Then, I hooked a leg over the top of the wall. From my perch, I stared out into the darkness beyond the tower.

I swallowed hard. A sense of loss pierced me for a moment.

I'd gone soft, that was all. And the longer I stayed in luxury, the easier I'd be to kill.

I stared across the paved expanse before me, focusing on the farthest dark point I could see. Shadow magic whispered up my spine and slid over my skin like a layer of frost. My cold breath iced the air. I jumped, my teeth chattering. I felt exhilarated and untethered at the same time.

From Tower Hill, I jumped through the shadows, moving further north. I rushed along what had once been the eastern edge of London's Roman wall, flying through the shadows. A gnawing pit had opened up in my chest, worsening the further I got from the Institute, but I kept moving. I always had to keep moving. Rest meant death. Hesitation meant death.

When I reached Leadenhall, I took a left. In the middle of the night, in this ancient part of the city, no one lingered on the streets. And even if I happened to pass some drunk banker lost in the city, he'd feel nothing more than the whoosh of cold air as I slipped past him.

I wasn't a Shadow Fae, but I could kill in the shadows, now, too.

At last, I reached Guildhall. Thousands of years ago, the Romans had ruled the city. They'd built a wall, temples, an amphitheater. And they'd left their ruins deep underground.

Baleros had taken their foundations and built from them, creating his own empire. Once, when I hadn't performed like he'd wanted me to in the ring, he'd locked me up for a week with only water. When I got out, crazed with starvation, I'd called him evil. I'd wanted to see if he had any sense of shame. He'd told me that good and evil didn't mean anything anymore. He said that wasn't the way the world worked. He'd said empire-builders created their own realities, and that for men like him, it had always been that way.

In the shadows near Guildhall, I pulled the cover off a manhole, and I jumped down. I splashed in the water, landing hard. The remains of the ancient Walbrook River reached about mid-calf. Long ago—even before the Romans had come—the noble Mor made sacrifices here. Now, the Shadow Fae had found another way to appease the Old Gods: with the blood of the demons they assassinated.

Shivering—why the hells was I so cold?—I rammed my hand into my backpack and pulled out my head-lamp. Rats scurried along the sides of the river. They didn't bother me. I'd spent enough time living with rats.

A circular, white glare from my headlamp bounced over the water and wet walls as I moved deeper through the river. The water froze my legs. It felt like gods-damned winter down here.

At last, I reached a fork where a narrow tunnel curved right. This would take me where I needed to go.

As I walked, shivers overtook me. I tried not to think about Ruadan, but a mixture of guilt and fear clouded my thoughts. Honestly, you'd think I could pick one or the other. Either he was a ruthless killer who would probably execute me or he genuinely liked me, and … oh, who was I kidding? Even if he liked me, any rational person would slaughter someone who'd betrayed them that way. It was just the way of the world.

The water grew shallower as I walked, the splashing quieter, until the river petered out into a dull trickle. A few minutes later, I reached the end of the tunnel. A wooden door—painted green—was inset into the brick here. A padlock sealed it shut.

I reached into my bag, pulling out two bobby pins. I bent one of them into a pick, and the other into a lever. I slid them both into the keyhole, jiggling them around until I unlocked it.

Before I pushed through the door, I flicked off my headlamp. I tucked the lumen crystal inside my shirt, disguising it within my cleavage. No need to broadcast my shadow-leaping ability.

Always let your enemy underestimate you.

Holding my breath, I carefully inched the door open, relieved when darkness greeted me.

My relief was short-lived as the smell of the old gladiator ring hit me. The stones, the sand. The only thing missing was the metallic stench of blood, or the overpowering smell of sweat. It made me want to vomit.

I moved silently over the sand, sniffing the air. I didn't need my headlamp to find my way into the center of the ring.

The arena was so dark, so quiet, that for a moment, I wondered if I'd got it wrong. Maybe Baleros wasn't here at all. Maybe he'd never remain somewhere so obvious.

I sniffed. When I picked out his rosewater scent, my heart skipped a beat. He was here.

I pulled my iron knife from its sheath. Shadows were all around me, but I didn't yet know where to jump.

I sniffed the air again. Roses.

He was so close. I could almost hear him—

Iron clamped around my throat, and the back of my head slammed hard into a wooden stake behind me. Metal creaked, and my lungs burned. I was choking, and I couldn't even scream.

My vision swam with dots.

I already knew what this was—Baleros's garrote. I couldn't speak as he tightened it. This was how the Romans had killed their worst enemies—a humiliating death, not even fighting. Baleros had used it to keep us all in line.

A revelation hit me like a train. He'd been waiting for me.

Of course he had. He was Baleros, and he lived in my head.

He turned the garrote again, and the world slipped away from me.

I'D LOST CONSCIOUSNESS, but when I regained it, I was staring up into the face of my old master. He'd flicked on my headlamp, and it shone brightly over his features. His eyes crinkled at the corners—genuine delight.

I wasn't sure how long I'd been out, but my mouth

felt like sandpaper, and the iron garrote seared my neck. Poison. The iron sapped my strength, and I wanted nothing more than to get it away from me.

I snarled at Baleros, and the fucker laughed.

As my vision slowly cleared, I took in the shapes around us. It took me a moment to realize we weren't alone. But it wasn't Ciara I found in the arena with us. It was an entire crowd of spectators, filling the stone seats. Excited murmurs rippled off the stone. What the fuck…?

Even more disturbing, a circle of archers lined the edge of the arena, each with a flaming arrow pointed right at me. A tendril of panic coiled through my chest.

I'd certainly gotten myself into a pickle.

"Arianna, my dear," said Baleros. "I was hoping you'd arrive."

I gritted my teeth. "How did you know I'd come for you?"

"I didn't, precisely. But I know how you think, and I prepared for all eventualities—one of them being your arrival in the arena. I thought, sometimes that girl does my bidding at first, then the naughty rebellious streak emerges, and she thinks she can take me on. This was merely one of the possible outcomes, but I was prepared." An easy smile lit up his face. "Please forgive me for knocking you unconscious. I needed a bit of time to prepare. But I think you'll agree that the results are spectacular. One final fight for the Amazon Terror." He loosed a long sigh. "I thought you would have learned by now. You can never win."

My mind was foggy from dehydration and the iron burning me. I couldn't make sense of this. What the fuck was his endgame?

"I don't understand." I hated not understanding. Hated that he was always one step ahead. "Why did you send me after the key in the first place? Why not just drag me back into the ring if you wanted me to fight?"

He shrugged. "Because I wanted you to fight someone very hard to capture. You never lose. Now, you will."

Baleros stepped aside, and my world tilted. There, on the other side of the ring, stood Ruadan. The arena lights gilded his body, and he gripped a sword. His eyes had darkened to pure black, and his teeth were gritted with sheer, murderous rage.

I was supposed to fight him. "You wanted the Wraith to track me here so we could fight."

"No one can capture him. Not even me. I had to lure him to me. You were the bait."

"And you don't want the key? You just want a fight between us?" I didn't believe him. He was simply making the best of the situation, getting everything he could out of it. He wanted a fight *and* the key.

"I don't need the key," he said. "And now that I know what it is, that it's a part of him... It's too complicated. Look, I simply thought, why not make money one last time? Do you know how much people paid to see the Wraith take on the Amazon Terror?"

He was lying. I knew he wanted nothing more than to unleash anarchy once more. He was desperate for the key. Before Ruadan got the chance to jump away, before even the Wraith saw what was coming, Baleros would shoot his limbs full of iron arrows. Baleros still didn't know what the key looked like, but he'd try to torture the answer out of Ruadan. Just before he killed him.

My hands were at the iron garrote around my neck. "What if we simply don't fight each other?"

He opened his hands. "You don't have a choice, my little monster. Ruadan wants you dead. He can shadow-jump. You can't. You may not last long, unfortunately, but the crowd wants blood, and they'll have it." He frowned at me. "I like the headlamp on you. I think I'll leave it."

I could still feel the lumen crystal tucked in my cleavage, and a spark of hope lit in my chest. Inwardly, I smiled. Baleros had no idea that I had it on me.

I fought hard to keep the fear etched across my features. If he didn't know about my skills, he hadn't planned for them. That gave me an advantage.

"There is one way you can win." He scratched his cheek. "If you unleash that dark power within you. You know, the one that terrifies you. The one you can't control. I've seen you do things that no fae should be able to do."

My mind flashed with an image from my past, one I wanted to keep buried. Twelve dead fae lying at my feet, their bodies rotting before my eyes.

I clenched my jaw tighter. "You'd better hope I don't

unleash that, Baleros. Because you'll die along with the rest of them."

He stroked the back of his fingertips along my cheeks, and I shuddered at his touch. There was a time when I would have welcomed it—any affection from him.

"My little monster, Arianna. A pretty, scarred little abomination." A sly smile. Charming, almost. "Arianna. But that's not your real name, is it?"

His words slid through my bones. If he told anyone....

I pushed the fear to the back of my mind. I had one more question for him. "How did you know I'd bring Ruadan here? How did you know I wouldn't kill him?"

A dark smile curled his lips. "Because you're pathetic, Arianna. When you're not busy murdering people, you're desperate for love. And all it would take was one tiny gesture of kindness to destroy your ability to think rationally. One little butterscotch sweet." He cocked his head, amusement dancing in his eyes. "What was it, Arianna? Some food? One of the lollipops you like so much?" He grinned at this like it was the funniest fucking thing he'd ever heard.

It was a blanket.

A wild rage roiled in my blood, so intense I thought I might explode and bring the world down with me, and the possibility was more real than I wanted to admit. "Someday, I will kill you. Slowly. And while you're dying, I will make you regret the day you pulled me off the streets of London. I am the Amazon Terror, and I will be your death." My voice was so cold, so full of wrath, that just for an instant, he flinched, and fear flickered across his face. It only took him a moment to compose himself.

He wasn't smiling anymore, and he stepped away from me. But the one little flash of fear had given me the insight I needed. Baleros had made himself into a god because he was afraid. He feared pain. And if he had enough power, he imagined he'd never have to feel anything that hurt.

If you stare into the abyss long enough, the abyss stares back at you.

He backed away from me, and he signaled to someone to open the garrote around my neck.

Then, Baleros turned to face the crowd, lifting his arms above his head like a circus ringmaster. "You've all heard of the fearsome skill of the Amazon Terror. She may look like a beautiful lavender-haired fae with tremendous breasts—"

He always mentioned the breasts in his preamble. The crowds loved breasts.

"—but she has left the bodies of countless warriors at her feet. She now faces the first enemy she may be unable to defeat. A spell-slayer. The Wraith. He moves in the shadows, slaughters silently. Ladies and gentlemen, I give you the fight you've all been waiting for!"

Someone handed me a bottle of water, and I chugged it down fast. My throat felt like a desert, and apparently Baleros wanted this battle to last a little longer than four seconds.

I stared across the sandy arena at Ruadan while the familiar proceedings began—the ancient customs marking the start of combat. The licti—servants—carried a bundle of sticks with an ax. That was the fascia—it was supposed to represent Baleros's power. My guess was it was there to compensate for a super disappointing manhood.

Then, the frankly irritating trumpeters blared away. Last, a servant held aloft a bust of Baleros that everyone was supposed to cheer for.

The entire time, my gaze was locked on Ruadan. Inky shadows slid through his eyes, and darkness breathed around him. He stood firmly in place with that eerie, animal stillness, bar a lock of pale blond hair that floated on a breeze. A predator about to attack. The sight of him sent ice racing through my veins. The ancient part of my brain was already screaming at me to run. I'd fought many enemies, but none as terrifying as him.

Unlike Baleros, Ruadan probably realized I'd stolen the lumen crystal, which meant he wouldn't mess around. He could shadow-jump faster and more skillfully than I could.

I gripped my sword tighter, my mind whirling. We could stall, trying to find a way to get out of this together. If we teamed up, maybe we could both live.

Or, we could assume the other person was a monster and go for the kill right away. After all, he was the Wraith. And I'd just stabbed him in the chest. Ruthless monsters, both of us.

Sweat dampened my palms as my mind frantically spun in a million directions. To trust him or not to trust him….

One of the licti commanded us to raise our weapons and salute our master. I turned to Baleros—seated on the stony emperor's throne in the center of the audience. I raised my sword without thinking—an old habit.

As I lowered it again, I knew that, one way or another, it would be the last time I saluted my old master.

My heart pounded rhythmically in my chest, beating in time to the war drum that signaled the start of the fight. And with a final trumpet's blare, it was time for the carnage to begin.

CHAPTER 30

$\mathcal{T}$ime seemed to slow down, and I stared at Ruadan, at his terrifying stillness.

Tonight, I fight a demigod.

Neither of us moved. I wasn't sure I was even breathing. Ruadan just stared back at me, his eyes black as the void. Dread clamped bony fingers around my heart.

I calculated where he would land if he shadow-jumped, realizing that the glaring lights cast my silhouette in front of me, not behind. If I could try to stay facing this direction, it would help me know what was coming.

Conversely, Ruadan's shadow was behind him. *Maybe* I could jump behind him and end this now....

Battle fury was already trembling through my limbs, making my legs shake. Complete silence shrouded the arena.

And yet, I just kept standing there. Waiting. My

blood roared in my ears, and tension rippled off the crowd as they grew restless.

Then, in a blur of black, Ruadan jumped—whirling through the air, just enough time for panic to steal my breath. He landed just in front of me. But instead of simply running his sword through me, he swung for me, aiming for the shoulder. Just like he always did.

I parried, our swords clashing, sparking in the air. We circled, swords slamming ferociously. I knew his rhythms, knew where he'd strike. And he knew mine. When I swung for him, he ducked, just like I knew he would. My sword whooshed over his head.

The audience bayed for blood.

From the ground, he swung for my legs, and I leapt into the air. Then, with a vicious strike, I snarled and slammed my sword into his blade so brutally that I knocked it from his hands. He jumped, landing in front of me, and clamped his hand hard around my throat, lifting me into the air. I dropped my sword, but I brought my knee up hard into his chin, his jaw cracking.

The crowd roared their approval.

He dropped me, and I slammed my fist into his stomach with all my might.

Good. With the swords out of the way. I might even get the chance to say something to him. Something like, *Baleros wants to kill you, so let's get out of this together. Sorry again for the stabbing.*

Ruadan was only down for a moment, and then his hands clamped down hard on my waist. He lifted me into the air, and the crowd screamed for death. Then, he threw me across the sandy pit, and I landed hard on my back. As I started to push myself up, his foot smashed into my ribs.

Well, he was giving them a good show, but I wasn't dead. That meant he was holding back.

Unless … unless he really just wanted to kick my arse all over the arena before he killed me.

I blocked out the pain wracking my body. From the ground, I lifted my hips, hitting him hard with a brutal side kick into his knee. Another kick, my heel slamming into the same knee. He faltered. When I jumped to my feet again, I stepped in close, planting one foot behind him. I swept his legs, and he slammed down onto his back.

I leapt onto him, straddling him, and I hammered him with punches—until he caught my fist. He snarled, canines bared, then started to crush my hand. With his iron grip, he twisted my arm until I shifted off him, landing face down in the dirt.

In the next moment, he was on top of me, a powerful arm hooked around my throat. He was going to choke me out.

He leaned in close.

Then, he whispered in my ear.

"I'm not going to kill you."

It was the first time I'd heard his voice, the rich, velvety timbre, and it sent my pulse racing.

I reached behind my head, grabbing at his arms, pretending like I was struggling. "I'm not going to kill you, either," I whispered. "But Baleros is. He wants the World Key."

I elbowed him hard in the face. Maybe we weren't going to kill each other, but we didn't want Baleros to catch on. I started to get up, and he pinned me down from the front this time, still straddling me.

Then, I thrust my pelvis up hard with all my force, knocking him off me. I scrambled up. Before I could even fully right myself, Ruadan hurtled into me. He knocked me hard to the ground, just managing to cushion the blow of my head against the floor with his hand. Quite the gentleman.

The crowd screamed, demanding a sacrifice.

Grandson of the Night God.

He was between my legs, and I stared up at his pure black eyes.

He controlled the shadows.

"Make it dark," I whispered. "I will find Baleros."

Without another word, frosted night magic burst from him, ripples of shadows that snuffed out the candles around us. I flicked off my headlamp as the shadows slid over the flaming arrows, dimming their flames until darkness reigned.

Screams erupted all over the arena.

Anarchy is the opportunity to remake the world the way we want it.

Baleros knew how to rule in chaos. And now, so did I. I knew this arena like the back of my hand.

In the darkness, I shadow-leapt to the emperor's

seat before Baleros had a chance to escape. I sniffed the air. Roses. The scent that always made me sick.

I'd found him, and he had no idea I was here.

I gripped him by the collar, then reared back my arm, punching him over and over in the face with all my strength, so hard I was sure I was breaking my own fist. He caught one of my punches, but fury whipped through me, and I brought my knee up hard into his groin.

He'd never seen me coming. He'd had no idea Ruadan would give me the lumen crystal, or that we'd refuse to kill each other. Baleros had never prepared for this.

The man had spent years drilling all of his thoughts into my mind. He'd studied me, learning how I worked, anticipating everything I'd done. Knowing my weaknesses. I was his monster, and he controlled me.

But it was like he always said—if you stare too long into the abyss, the abyss stares back at you. He knew how I thought, and I knew how he thought, too.

I rammed my elbow into his face, and he moaned. "Ruadan...."

"I'm not Ruadan," I roared. "I'm the abyss, bitch!"

I'm not sure that made sense, and maybe I needed a better catchphrase. But it felt right in the moment.

"Where's Ciara?" I screamed.

He tried to hit me, but I was blocking his blows. Then, I jabbed my fingers swiftly into his Adam's apple. He emitted a choking sound, unable to breathe, and I

shadow-jumped behind him. I gripped his head—
Ruadan-style—ready to snap his neck.

"Where's Ciara?" I shouted. "Do not make me rip
out your spine, because I will, fucker."

Screams tore through the air around us, but Ruadan
was keeping a tight control of the shadows. Darkness
claimed the arena.

As soon as Baleros could speak again, he groaned,
"Secret location."

"Where?" I roared.

"I brought her here tonight. Your cage," he
choked out.

I snapped his neck, and he went down. Without
iron in my hands, I couldn't kill him now. I had to leave
for Ciara while I still could, but I hoped to hell that
Ruadan would drive an iron sword through his heart.

I leapt through the darkness, the arena air rushing
over my skin. Just before I rushed into the exit, I
whirled to look behind me. A burst of light flashed in
the arena as Ruadan's darkness receded for just a
moment. It was just enough time to watch as Ruadan
cut his sword through Baleros's neck. My heart leapt.

As Baleros's body fell, it erupted into flames, and
the scent of charred flesh filled the air. *Dead.* My breath
caught in my lungs.

I had no idea why his body had ignited. I only knew
it was all over, although I almost couldn't believe it.

I spun, leaping through the tunnel again. Baleros
might be dead, but he had dozens of lackeys working
for him here.

Baleros's thirty-fourth law of power: never let down your guard.

My heart slammed against my ribs. Maybe his body was dead, but he'd be living on in my mind for a while.

I LEAPT THROUGH THE DARKNESS, knowing exactly where to find Ciara. I knew these tunnels intimately, and with the lumen crystal, it only took me a few seconds to get there. He'd brought her here tonight. What if I'd gone straight for the cages instead of into the arena? He wasn't worried, because he was convinced I'd act exactly as he'd predicted.

At last, I reached the damp cavern where I'd once lived. A flood of memories washed over me, the dank scent and dripping water making bile rise in my throat. I'd given six years of my life to this hole.

Dead. It was hard to wrap my mind around it. Baleros's presence was still a living thing in my mind.

At this point, I remembered I was still wearing my headlamp, and I flicked it on.

There, curled up in the bottom of the cage, was Ciara.

She sat up, squinting in the bright light, her face covered in dirt.

"Ciara! It's me."

"Arianna?" Dehydration had paled her lips and cheeks.

I pulled my homemade lock pick out of my pocket

and jammed it into the lock. "I'm getting you out of here. Now." After a few seconds of fiddling, the lock clicked. With a racing pulse, I ripped off the padlock. "Baleros is dead."

"You killed him," she shrieked with joy, beaming.

"No. The Wraith did."

"I don't care who killed him, as long as he's dead." She blinked at the headlamp. "How the heck did you manage to find me?"

"The Wraith and I did the one thing Baleros never would have anticipated. Something he'd never begin to understand."

"What?"

"We trusted each other." I grabbed her hand. "Come on. We need to get out of here."

Baleros had never anticipated that Ruadan would trust me enough to give me the crystal. He'd never imagined we'd work together to survive, because that wasn't how Baleros thought.

I pulled Ciara along as we ran through the dark tunnel, our feet pounding hard over the dirt. Mentally, I calculated our next move.

Ruadan and I had worked together, but that didn't mean the Institute would forgive me for what I'd done. Did they know? Had someone found Ruadan and pulled the knife from his chest? I wasn't sticking around London long enough to find out. I had a pretty strong feeling I was on Grand Master Savus's shit list. Also known as his kill list.

I didn't think I'd exactly be welcome at the Institute at this point.

Ciara's breath heaved. "Where are we going?"

"We're getting out of London, Ciara. We're going into hiding."

At last, we reached the part of the tunnel where only a steel manhole cover blocked our exit. I hoisted Ciara up until she could push it to the side, and we hauled ourselves out into the London night.

Within minutes, we were disappearing into the night's shadows.

CHAPTER 31

J sat across from Ciara, in a dark corner of a pub in Edinburgh. The bar was indistinct, just like I wanted it to be. Ordinary wooden tables, an old carpet with wine stains, plain yellow walls. We'd spent twenty of our last pounds on haggis and neeps, which had been a mistake, because it was disgusting. Of course Ciara loved it.

In the past few days since we'd run from London, I'd made myself look as nondescript as possible. I wore a hood or wig to cover my lavender hair. I wore jeans and sneakers. I didn't make eye contact with anyone. No one had noticed us.

Problem was, we were running out of Ciara's money, fast.

Ciara leaned back in her chair, sipping her beer. "We have twenty-six pounds and thirteen pence left."

I swallowed hard. I still had the lumen crystal. It

wouldn't be particularly difficult to steal from people. "I'll find us what we need."

She leaned in closer to me, whispering, "You said Baleros's headless body just caught on fire? He was a devil. I knew it."

"No doubt about that. I hope it hurt."

She shoved a forkful of haggis into her mouth, chewing thoughtfully, her gaze intent on her food. "Why did you run from Ruadan? I thought you said you worked together to kill Baleros."

I swirled the wine in my glass. "We did work together in that moment, to get out of that situation. To save both our lives. But I don't know what it means. Grand Master Savus calls the shots in the Institute, and I don't know what he thinks. I could be on a kill list. I stole from them. And I stabbed one of them. And the Shadow Fae really don't have a sense of humor about those kind of things."

"You took something from me." A rich, velvet voice sent ice racing through my blood.

It was a voice I'd heard before.

Only once before—in the arena.

My mouth went dry, and I turned to find Ruadan looming over us. His bright violet eyes looked striking against the gloom of the bar.

"Ruadan!" I tried to sound cheerful. "I was just talking about you."

He stared at me with that preternatural stillness. For just a moment, a chill rippled over me, but it was gone within an instant. If he'd wanted to kill me, he would have done it by now.

A hush fell over the bar as the humans began to realize a powerful fae warrior stood in their midst. So much for discretion.

"Why don't we talk outside?" I said.

He nodded once.

I ignored everyone's wide-eyed stares as we crossed outside. Clouds covered the moon tonight, and a light rain misted on the old, winding street. From where we stood, I could see all the way up to Edinburgh Castle, a gothic palace on jagged slopes.

"So. You want your crystal back?" I asked.

He pressed his hands against the wall, boxing me in. His glare cut right through me. Silver glinted in his eyes. "How did Baleros compel you to enter the Institute?"

Knowledge gives you power over a person. How much power did I want Ruadan to have? I supposed my life was already in his hands right now. How much worse could it get? Still, I'd leave out the key details.

"How did he get anyone to do anything?" I asked. "He had leverage. Nothing made me happier than to see you cut his head off."

A gust of wind whipped at his hair, and an eerie stillness overtook his body.

"Am I on the kill list?" I asked.

No answer. Just dark shadows whipping the air around him. The bastard had already broken his vow, but he preferred brooding in silence and generally trying to scare the crap out of people.

"I'm sorry I stabbed you," I added. "Honestly, *stabbed* sounds a bit dramatic. You're a demigod and a fae. I knew you'd live if I didn't use iron. I mean, for a minute I did consider...." I was nervously babbling, filling the silence with things that would get me in trouble. "You know what? Let's not dwell on what might have been. I'm alive. You're alive. Baleros is dead. Let's try to keep it that way."

Even though The Wraith stood before me, his magic crackling the air, I didn't feel threatened right now. I felt an overwhelming urge to close the distance between us, to press myself against his powerful chest. I took a step closer to him, breathing in. There—under the pine and the magic, the scent of apples. I loved that smell. I closed my eyes, inhaling again, and that's when I realized where I knew it from. It was the one from my dreams.

I frowned at him. "Have you ever heard of a place called Emain, by any chance?"

He cut me a sharp look, eyes darkening. "No."

The look in his eyes told me he was lying.

"You're not as good a liar as you think you are. What's the big deal about it? I've dreamt of it. One of the library books says dreaming of Emain is a fae thing. Also that it's the headquarters of all the Shadow Fae. You smell like my dreams." I cleared my throat. "Which sounds more like a pickup line than I'd intended."

His gaze flicked up and down my body, as if he

were still considering something. "It's a myth. Don't speak of it again."

Right. Convincing. "So, am I on the kill list?" I asked again.

The cool breeze kissed my skin while his gaze bored into me.

At last, he said, "No. I don't think you are. I'm coming back for you. The Institute hasn't finished with you."

My chest unclenched, and I released the breath I'd been holding. "Are you going to tell me why you've suddenly become a chatty Cathy?"

"I can speak again because I've completed my mission."

I nodded slowly. "Killing Baleros?"

"In the arena, I thought you were going to do it. You left him alive. Why?"

I really wasn't used to the sound of him talking, and his voice was having a distracting effect on me. In fact, its richness seemed to skim over my skin and stroke my body in places I shouldn't be thinking about right now. No wonder he didn't talk.

A long silence stretched out between us. I wasn't sure I trusted him enough to tell him how much Ciara meant to me. "There was something else I had to do," was all I said.

Before I could ask another one of the hundreds of questions burning in my head, he turned, prowling off.

I watched as he stalked into Edinburgh's shadows, blending in with the night itself.

I touched my throat, realizing that he'd left me with the lumen stone. As he walked away, that faint scent of apples hung in the air, and I felt an unfamiliar sense of safety. Did the demonic Wraith actually make me feel safe now?

Surprise flickered in my chest as I realized I was looking forward to his return.

With a sharp pang, it made me think of something that hardly ever popped into my mind these days. A place I'd nearly forgotten on the dirt floor of Baleros's cages.

Home.

I pushed the thought away. Home was an impossibility, now, and I'd never find my way back. Now, Ciara was my home. When I crossed back into the pub and found that she'd saved half her disgusting haggis for me, warmth lit up my chest.

I beamed at her. "What are you smiling at?" she asked.

"You." I sat back down in my chair. "Giving me food. Sometimes a butterscotch sweet is a genuine gift."

"Right. I remember how obsessed you were with butterscotch sweets—that one you hung onto forever in the cage because you didn't want it to be gone. I need to get you a whole bag."

I shook my head. "I don't even like how it tastes. I don't like haggis, either. I just like that you gave it to me."

"You're a weird one, Arianna."

I reached into my bug-out bag, pushing the headlamp and duct tape out of the way until I found a grape lollipop, then I popped it into my mouth. "I don't know what you mean."

* * *

COURT OF DARKNESS, the second book in the series, is available.

Thanks so much for reading our books.

Also, please join our Reader group to discuss Court of Shadows and other books!

www.cncrawford.com

ACKNOWLEDGMENTS

Thanks to my supportive family, and to Michael Omer for his fantastic feedback and help managing my many author crises. Thanks to Nick for his insight and help crafting the book.

Robin Marcus and Isabella Pickering are my fabulous editors. Thanks to my advanced reader team for their help, and to C.N. Crawford's Coven on Facebook!

Made in the USA
Middletown, DE
03 February 2024

49072617R00163